WALTER BENJAMIN

STARES AT THE SEA

STORIES BY C.D. ROSE

MELVILLE HOUSE
BROOKLYN · LONDON

T0034921

WALTER BENJAMIN STARES AT THE SEA

First published in 2024 by Melville House
Copyright © 2023 by C. D. Rose
All rights reserved
First Melville House Printing: November 2023

Melville House Publishing
46 John Street
Brooklyn, NY 11201
and
Melville House UK
Suite 2000
16/18 Woodford Road
London E7 0HA

mhpbooks.com
@melvillehouse

ISBN: 978-1-68589-084-1
ISBN: 978-1-68589-085-8 (eBook)

Library of Congress Control Number: 2023945611

Designed by Beste M. Doğan

Printed in the United States of America
10 9 8 7 6 5 4 3 2 1

A catalog record for this book is available from the Library of Congress

WALTER BENJAMIN STARES AT THE SEA

ALSO BY C. D. ROSE

The Blind Accordionist

The Biographical Dictionary of Literary Failure

Who's Who When Everyone Is Someone Else

I confess I do not believe in time. I like
to fold my magic carpet, after use, in such a way
as to superimpose one part of the
pattern upon another. Let visitors trip.
—VLADIMIR NABOKOV

If we could but separate kairos, a
moment in time, from chronos, its flow, everything
would become known to us.
—LUCREZIA FINTA

Time is a river that sweeps me away, but I am the
river; it is a tiger that destroys me, but I am the tiger;
it is a fire that consumes me, but I am the fire.
—JORGE LUIS BORGES

I like things that flicker.
—ANGELA CARTER

STORIES

WALTER BENJAMIN

STARES AT THE SEA

OGNOSIA

Leidner's train pulled in around four, too early and too late to do anything useful, so he walked the couple of miles across town to the hotel and by late afternoon was happily sitting in the back bar, a place he found familiar even though he'd never been there before. All alcoves and corners, worn seats at wide tables, narrow windows onto a side street, and dark stairwells: such places were where he belonged.

He made sure he had his back to the wall so he could see who was coming or going, set his notebook on the table, checked the battery in his phone (if the interviewee was a talker he'd need the voice recorder), then flicked through the book they'd couriered to him. It wasn't his beat, but their regular hack was double-booked. The money would be handy, too.

'Have a look at the pictures, ask some questions, two thousand words by next Monday,' his editor had said. 'You'll recognise her when she walks in.'

Leidner was still getting over the train ride, which had been marked by an uncomfortable misrecognition. A man across the aisle had been reading a book and Leidner had squinted to see what it was, an old habit, but he couldn't make out the title, then looked up to see the man looking back at him. For a tenth of a second they shared a glance as though they might know each other, but they didn't. The person Leidner was thinking of lived a thousand miles away and, besides, was also dead.

This book was heavy, 120 pages of 200 gsm paper, the size of an LP. There were a couple of introductory essays, which he ignored, then the pictures. Each one (colour, full page) showed a scene set but not yet occupied. An anonymous motorway sliproad at dawn, or maybe dusk; a provincial railway station, a goods yard to its side, the tracks cutting through the frame; banked rows of plush red-velvet theatre seats, then the reverse angle—an empty stage. Each photo was a place waiting for something to happen. A small study or office centred on a desk piled with books, spines illegible; a blustery seascape; more empty streets. There were no people. Leidner found them cold, pointless. Great composition, great light, but what else? What were these pictures supposed to mean? Then the last one: It was this place. The hotel bar he was sitting in now. His seat by the window empty. All of it empty. As though the picture had been taken but a few hours earlier.

He looked up to see if he could work out the exact angle or spot the photo had been taken from, and as he was scanning the room he again saw someone, not the same guy from the train, he thought he remembered but could not place. It was today's thing, obviously. Leidner took a deep breath, looked away, wanting to avoid the jitters, the worries, the anxieties that came with the thought that everything might be connecting in a way he wouldn't like at all, then looked back to find the man was still looking directly at him, though actually he wasn't looking at Leidner at all but merely staring into the middle distance, rapt at a memory of the point in his life when he had been happiest. This had been some time ago, in the late '90s or early noughties maybe, sitting on a beach, alone. Das had been working as a teacher and had taken a group of Spanish students on a day trip to the seaside then managed to give them all the slip, leaving them in an amusement arcade while he wandered off with the vague idea of getting a beer and sitting in the sun. He'd ended up on the beach instead with a cheese sandwich, some loose change, and nothing much else. He listened to the crunch of the pebbles under the weight of the tide, watched the light bouncing off the waves, and thought that his heart might burst for no reason other than that he was there, and alive, and when he had realised that he might never be happier this fact made him sad, as though the wave had crested.

The moment had never left him, and today he had gone back there, to the very place where it had happened, in an attempt to find it again. His old mate Griff was getting married for the third time and there was a stag. Das hadn't wanted to go even though they'd promised it would be a quiet one, but when he saw it was there, in that place where he'd been so happy all that time ago and had never been back, he thought again. He'd get there early, go down to the beach, find the exact spot, and have his moment again. Only it hadn't

worked that way: he hadn't been able to find the place, or even anything like it. The beach wasn't the same one he remembered at all—
not the long expanse of sand-coloured pebbles and blue water but a
narrow strip of grubby sand hemmed in by an industrial port. Das
wondered if he'd got the place wrong, if it hadn't been here but somewhere else, and if his memory had been faulty or blurred all these
years, if it had overlapped with one or two or more other incidents,
if his perfect moment of stillness had never, in fact, happened at all.

He checked his phone again to see if any of the others were on
their way yet as much as to avoid the gaze of the guy sitting by the
window, now staring at him in a way that was almost creepy, then set
it to ring in an hour's time, then two hours, then three. He'd never
been able to put up with the group of honking bores any gathering
of more than three men inevitably became, especially if booze was
involved. The phone trick was simple: a faked incoming call that he'd
get up to answer, then go outside, then drift off and disappear completely. That lot would be bladdered within the hour, grown both
bullish and maudlin. They'd not notice him gone for ages, if at all.

Das saw himself walking into the cooler night air, cadging a
cigarette off a stranger, striking up a conversation, going on somewhere else entirely, a club, maybe, where they'd be playing thump-
ing techno and he'd get talking to someone glamorous dressed in
black and he'd get close to them and go back to theirs, that was how
it would happen, then he'd wake up the next morning in a strange
place, in an unfamiliar bed that would be too comfortable, ashamed,

or maybe not, maybe in love again, and he'd have to explain to everyone how he'd met this person who'd come into his life like this, he'd
tell the story of how he'd been on a stag do then wandered off, but it
wouldn't last because—

'Sir, are you okay? Sir?'

'What?'

'Sir, are you okay?' Lena had only just started her shift and really couldn't be doing with crying drunks this early on a long night,
especially when she was going out later and had a big one planned.

'You didn't look very well. Is everything all right?'

'Sorry, no. Sorry. I'm okay, thanks. Fine. Sorry.'

Turned out the guy wasn't drunk after all, just lost. It happened. Lena felt as though she'd intruded and backed off, leaving
the man to dab his tears with a paper napkin. It'd be at least an hour
before she could sneak out for a smoke.

There were two groups booked in later, but for the while it was
quiet. Lena hoped Zan would turn up soon, as she was on her own
at the moment and wouldn't be able to cope with the rush. The tips
never made it worthwhile unless you flirted, and there was no way
she was doing that again. Lena was utterly uncut out to do this job.
She liked watching, but hated participating. Zan had told her that
she never got involved, that it was her default to avoid conflict, and
therefore people, because people *were* conflict, and that she couldn't
build a personality, a *life*, on conflict avoidance, so when Lena had
seen this rather forlorn man sitting there alone gently sobbing she'd

thought she ought to do something, get involved, communicate, conflict-avoid. Besides, he looked a little bit like her brother, who she hadn't seen in years.

She reached for the sketchbook in the pocket of her apron. It was kind of a habit, nothing more than doodles, really, perhaps more of a compulsion than a habit, this need to recreate faces, to note them, or record them, to put down something solid from the shifting mass. Zan had told her she should try selling her pictures, or showing them somewhere, but Lena didn't really get that, it wasn't why she did it. Zan had all sorts of ideas, like the scam, which had come to nothing because no one used cash anymore, not enough to make it worthwhile, anyhow, though now she had something involving phones that Lena was equally unsure about. Lena had only ever had one job that she'd considered 'proper,' and that had turned wrong after the boss had insisted on looking at her sketchbook, which, of course, had a fairly unflattering picture of him in it. The boss said it was funny, and that she was certainly talented, but Lena was fairly sure that was why, three months later, her contract hadn't been renewed.

She hoped it wouldn't get too busy before Zan turned up. Zan was always late. She hoped Zan would at least show before Rasputin did, anyhow. Rasputin came in every night and ordered one negroni with double Campari, which he nursed until closing. He had a disturbing stare and an exaggerated interest in Lena's tattoos. 'Which one of those do you regret?' he'd asked her. What sort of a fucking question was that? Zan would have had a smart answer; Lena's was 'None of them.'

Lena hadn't even managed to get the sketchbook out before someone else was calling her.

'Excuse me, have you seen my phone?'

'I'm sorry, I haven't. If anything's lost it gets handed in to the bar. I can go and ask if you like.' Lena was worried that this was something to do with Zan's scam and hoped it wasn't. Karsh, on the other hand, was more worried about how they'd get in touch with Ginny if Ginny didn't show soon as this was Film Club, after all, the one night each month they'd get together as they had been doing for the last ten years to go and see a film, and now Karsh had lost their phone and there was no sign of the usually punctual Ginny.

'Can you tell me what it's like?' asked the waiter, but Karsh couldn't remember anything more about the phone than it being black and shiny and phone-shaped and phone-sized, and right now was more taken by the fact that this waiter, shaved head apart, looked exactly like the actor in the film they were supposed to be going to see whose name they couldn't remember, nor what the film was called. It had been Ginny's turn to choose and as usual she'd chosen something art-house weirdy-beardy, not Karsh's thing at all, but that was how Film Club worked.

Karsh carried on looking at the waiter as she walked off to the bar, wondering if it was that actor she looked like or someone else altogether. It was an increasingly familiar feeling. Everyone was starting to look like everyone else these days. Same with the films: it didn't really matter which one of them picked; Karsh found they couldn't remember much about them half an hour after they'd finished. There'd been one grainy black-and-white thing, probably Ginny's choice, that had stuck with them, though if pushed they wouldn't be able to say why. Good job they had the Book: Karsh kept a record, had noted the title of every film they'd seen plus their thoughts on it and a mark out of ten in the notebook they had with them right now. Ginny made fun, but that was what Ginny did. Karsh dug in their bag, fished it out, and flicked through it, trying to remember what that one film was. Even reading it back didn't help much. None of the descriptions made much sense. They used to write them together when they went for a drink after. Film Club, Karsh knew, wasn't really about the films.

They reached for their phone again, only to remember they'd lost it. Never mind; Ginny was sure to show up soon. Karsh was always losing things these days, or forgetting them. There seemed to be so much more now, both things themselves and things to remember. No wonder it was getting harder to keep track of it all. The phone was supposed to help but had only made things even more complicated.

'Excuse me, do you know why you've been put on this earth?' Karsh looked up to find a woman with rinsed-out blonde hair looking at them intently. 'Why it is, I mean, that you're here?'

Karsh wondered if this was something else they were supposed to know and had forgotten again.

'I'm here,' they said, 'to meet a friend.'

'No, I mean, not tonight, I mean, like, *on this earth*. I mean, in a bigger way. Like, *really*.'

'We go and see films together. Once a month.' The woman looked like the kind of person who'd ask to speak to the manager. Trouble was, Karsh didn't have a manager. 'She's late, my friend. Should be here any minute. I think.'

The woman didn't seem to be listening, though. She was looking upward, as if she could see something but wouldn't tell anyone else about it. Karsh wondered if she was an evangelist or some other kind of proselytising fanatic, but that was unlikely in a place like this. Maybe just a hippy, or an eccentric. There was a man with her, though he was standing aside, as if embarrassed. She was clearly half-cut, thought Karsh, but she wasn't, Anja hadn't even had a drink yet, though she was waiting for her companion to go and get her one. Actually, Anja was thinking that she was disappointed by the fact that so few people had ever been able to answer her question. She'd taken to asking it of random strangers a few years ago, and it had done her little good. People thought she was aggressive, but she didn't mean to be. *Do you know why you've been put on this earth?* She was honestly just curious. She'd had her own moments of certainty: an intense but brief bout of religious faith when she was thirteen; deciding to live for rave when she was eighteen; finding herself in Goa by the time she was twenty and staying there for far too long, then somehow ending up working in corporate event management for nearly a decade. After that had collapsed, she'd developed the strong feeling that, in accordance with the ancient Mayan calendar, the world was due to end in 2012. When it hadn't, she'd had a bit of a reckoning. Now she genuinely wanted to know: *Why are we here?*

Anja had just asked the man she was with right now, who she'd met waiting to cross the street ten minutes ago, and whose name she didn't think she'd quite gathered, and he'd said that he didn't, no, but that he might like to talk about it over a drink, but he was already inching away from her by the time they'd got into the bar, she could tell, this wasn't a new thing. There was only one person who'd ever replied with certainty: a man she'd sat next to on a bus once. She'd asked the question, and instead of pretending it was his stop, he'd told her a long story about walking up a mountain and meeting God at the top. 'It was like a cloud coming down over my face,' he'd said. Anja couldn't remember much else about the story.

Her interviewee proving unforthcoming (Anja wondered if they were all there), Anja sat herself down in an alcove (there were so many of them here) next to a man to whom she'd intended to ask the question, but he seemed to be asleep. Gil wasn't quite asleep, though, but on the verge and starting to dream, and this was what he was dreaming: His lover was dancing happily to a punk band playing in the corner of a supermarket, and he felt happy because his lover had been troubled of late, it was good to see her so content, so he let her be and walked out onto a narrow English alley, which he took to be somewhere in Sussex (even though he'd never been to Sussex), then carried on and turned onto a Mediterranean esplanade, deserted,

lined by palm trees and pale yellow late-nineteenth-century buildings. A warm spray from the sea touched his face and an intense light
glowed around him. They should live here, Gil was thinking in the
dream, if only it weren't so expensive, and then someone was asking
him something, and he was waking somewhere else.

'Do you know why you've been put on this earth?'

Awake, Gil tried to recall the street where he'd felt so content,
unaware that the image he was trying to bring to mind was exactly
one of the pictures Leidner was looking at that very minute.

'Do we know each other?' he asked.

'Not yet,' Anja replied, and she reminded Gil of someone he'd
known when he'd been hauling sound systems around the free fes-
tival circuit, but he didn't like to think much of those days now, so
he turned away from her at the same time Anja had the same recognition, and she also didn't like to think about those times so also
turned away, which meant that they both saw that this place, this hotel bar, the evening dark starting to grow, was filled with tables each
with one person sitting at them, which was exactly the same as a photograph they had both seen at an exhibition some ten years earlier,
a picture that had stayed with them even though they didn't know
why, a picture that had been taken by Karsh when they had been
experimenting with photography and when they'd met Ginny, and a
picture that Lena had sometimes thought of drawing, Lena who was
now trying to take an order from a man who was rapidly realising
that he was in entirely the wrong place, having confused the name of

this bar with another, identical, in a town one hundred miles away. He noticed a tiny spider crawling over her hand and moved to brush it off but accidentally squashed it.

'I'll have to say a prayer to the Spider God now,' he said, 'asking for forgiveness,' and it reminded Lena of a stop-motion animation film about a spider that she had seen years ago and that had always given her the creeps, a film Das had seen, too, though he couldn't remember it at all.

And at that moment Gil's lover walked in and smiled at him, and he remembered exactly where the place he had dreamed was.

And Anja felt a cloud, not coming down over her, but lifting from her, as she realised why she was on this earth, though that realisation wouldn't have any effect for a few years yet.

And Karsh remembered it wasn't Film Club night at all so set off home, and on their way home realised they'd lost their keys but at the same moment remembered exactly who the actor or the waiter looked like and decided to try and get in touch with them again.

And Lena saw Zan walk in and smile at her, and it felt good, but though she knew she loved her, she also knew that she needed to stop their relationship right now, and after she'd done that she'd ditch the party and go to see the film that Karsh hadn't and think the actor in it did look a bit like her, and that she should perhaps grow her hair out, and find someone else, or maybe spend some time on her own, and felt like she was coming up on a pill she hadn't yet taken.

And Das got a call, too early for the one he'd set up, and thought it would be from one of the lads but it was an unknown number that he decided to answer anyway, and it wasn't a scam but Maddy, who he'd worked with that summer all those years ago and had hardly heard from again.

And Leidner sat there watching all this unfold, realising the pictures weren't of places waiting for things to happen but places where something had already happened.

The photographer arrived and sat down in front of him.

'Sorry I'm late,' she said.

'No problem,' he replied, then asked her what he really wanted to know.

'Well,' she said, 'that's a question, isn't it?'

THE DISAPPEARER

Louis Aimé Augustin Le Prince was born in Metz, close to the Franco-German border, in 1841. When only a small child, his father introduced him to Louis Daguerre, and the boy lost himself in the photographer's laboratory. Iodine, chlorine, bromine. The boy was in love. He disappeared there, for the first time. They found him hiding in the darkroom. The smell of chemicals stayed with him: aged eighteen he went to Leipzig to study chemistry and while there befriended John Whitley, scion of a Yorkshire engineering dynasty. On finishing his studies, Louis accepted his classmate's offer of a job in the family firm, and ended up with more than mere employment: in 1869, he married his best friend's twin sister, Elizabeth.

Strange that at such a moment—newlywed, a new career and home ahead of him—that Le Prince should disappear again. But disappear he did, as into the darkroom, for nearly two years. His name appeared on a regimental list, dated 1870: Le Prince had helped to defend Paris in the siege that marked the end of the Franco-Prussian war. This, only, is known. For the following year, including the two months of the Commune, his movements are obscure.

By 1871, however, he was in Leeds, working for his father-in-law's brass valve company and helping his wife to set up the Leeds Technical School of Art, an idea as radical and strange in that day as our own. The few students who enrolled later recalled little of Le Prince, remembering only a man constantly busied, if not troubled, by his work.

In 1881 the firm sent him to New York in pursuit of a contract. He spent most of the month-long voyage locked in his cabin, but sometimes, at night, he would walk the decks, staring at the dark horizon, trying to identify the scarcely visible line that divided sea from sky. Contract won, he opted not to return to Leeds, but instead sent for his family (now including three children). Over the next decade he travelled frequently back and forth across the Atlantic, though Elizabeth and the children stayed in New York. By 1889, he had decided to settle in America for good and set off for a final trip to Europe, returning to Leeds to conclude his affairs.

A year later he was still there, his business having taken longer than anticipated. Eventually ready to leave, feeling he would no longer return to Europe, he went to France. Two friends from Yorkshire accompanied Le Prince as far as Paris, where they stayed while Louis went on to Dijon to see his brother, a struggling architect. The reasons for his visit are far from clear, a final fond farewell, perhaps, an invitation to America, advice on how to run his business. A 'question relating to an inheritance' was mentioned by the friends, though from whom, to whom, and of how much is not known.

On September 16, 1890, Le Prince boarded a train in Dijon for Paris. He was due to meet his friends there, go back to Leeds, collect his belongings, then leave for New York, where his wife and children awaited him. He was never heard from again.

Five years to the day after Le Prince's second disappearance, two brothers who both worked for their father's photographic company headed south to visit the small port of La Ciotat, not far from Marseilles. If they'd been hoping for a beach holiday, they wouldn't have been lucky: even though it was September in a Mediterranean town, it was cold. You can see by the heavy clothes the people are wearing in the film the brothers made that day.

First shown at the end of 1895, the Lumières' *L'arrivée d'un train en gare de La Ciotat* is often called the earliest moving picture. Less than a minute long, a single unedited shot, *L'arrivée* certainly looks like the first modern film. The images move fluidly, no longer jerky flip-book photos, and the camera is placed close to the edge of the platform to best capture the velocity of the oncoming train. As the film begins the train is not visible, but it rapidly curves in, blurring slightly even in digital reproduction, then comes into extreme close-up as it meets the viewer face-to-face, still going too fast to stop, before skewering off, screen left, a trick. Once gone, we see the carriages halt quickly, dispersing a few passengers as others get on.

'Gare' is putting it strongly. There is no platform, no station building visible, no blue sign. There is bustle, a stationmaster. A few people glance briefly at the camera; most seem not to notice it.

The Lumière Brothers were unsure of what they had created, thinking they had discovered an interesting gimmick, an amusing modern gewgaw that they soon dropped in favour of colour photography. (Later, one of the brothers recorded his disappointment that people were more impressed by moving black-and-white images than static colour ones.)

The story goes, of course, that as the Lumières' train arrived on screen, audiences fled. One observer wrote how his neighbour howled in fear, then tried to hide under her seat (which seems a strange thing to do as protection against an oncoming train). This outbreak of panic has since been much doubted yet remains one of cinema's founding myths. The power of the moving image to simulate life and provoke wonder: Film is an art of disappearance. Traces of light pass across a surface, convincing the viewer that something is there, only to vanish. It promises that which it simultaneously denies.

Europeans think the Lumières invented cinema; Americans believe it was Edison. Muybridge, Eastmann, Bouly, Prószyński, Friese-Green, and Guy-Blaché, men and women with their kinetoscopes and dioramas, biophantic lanterns and chronophotographs, are almost entirely forgotten.

L'arrivée d'un train en gare de La Ciotat is part of the story that has effaced these others: no one is actually sure if it was first shown in 1895 or in 1896. It probably didn't cause panic. It certainly wasn't the first-ever moving picture.

The first-ever moving picture had already been made, nearly ten years earlier, by Louis Le Prince. In October 1888, on that brief trip back to Europe, Le Prince continued what he had been doing in America and carried out his most complete experiments with recorded moving images. In New York he had left the family firm and started running illuminated diorama shows while refining their technology, developing a single-lens camera from his original cumbersome sixteen-lens monster. Elizabeth, his wife, worked in a school for the deaf in Washington Heights, where by night Louis projected his images onto blank walls. (Marie, their youngest daughter, would later recall the nights she crept up to the large dark room where her father lost himself, closed in his work. She remembers watching huge shadows leap around the walls, cold flames, spirits.)

In 1886 Le Prince applied for a patent for his single-lens camera, apparently sensing only the potential market value of the machine itself, rather than that of hauling it around county fairs or travelling circuses, much less of opening a chain of screening rooms or cinemas (he never gave any public screenings or exhibitions of his invention.) Three years later he took dual French-US citizenship, believing it would make the process easier. Before the patent was granted, however, he made that last trip back to Europe to collect his machines, settle his affairs, and, almost incidentally, make that first-ever film.

Barely two seconds long, *Roundhay Garden Scene* shows Le Prince's son Adolphe together with members of the Whitley family self-consciously parading around the garden of a large house in a Leeds suburb. Less than two years before Le Prince's final train journey, it's impossible to watch these flickering people and not wonder what they know, and what we don't.

There are many theories regarding Le Prince's eventual end. The immediate hypothesis was that he had committed suicide. Financial difficulties, a failing marriage, perhaps. Who can fathom the motives of so many superficially successful suicides, that most effective of disappearances?

Yet it is not only the lack of motive that weakens this theory. How had Le Prince managed to leap out of a speeding train without a single witness? Perhaps he had not done himself in by jumping from the train but had simply slipped away at a provincial station, checked into a tatty hotel to slit his wrists, drink poison, or fashion a noose from a dirty sheet. Yet were this so, why was no body ever found? And, if he was about to commit suicide, why would he have taken his luggage with him?

He may have been the victim of an assault, murdered, and his luggage stolen. Again, the lack of witnesses gravitates against this, as well as the fact that Le Prince was six foot four, well-built, and probably handy in a fight.

By 1898 an American company, Mutuoscope, had built a camera based on Le Prince's model (possibly with the collaboration of Elizabeth and Adolphe, the eldest son) only to find itself arraigned by the notoriously litigious Edison Electric Company. Adolphe testified for Mutuoscope against Edison. Two years later, Adolphe was killed in a duck shooting accident on Fire Island.

Under English law, then as now, it was seven years before Le Prince could be declared legally deceased, and accordingly his effects were impounded until 1897. By the time anyone could get their hands on the camera, it was history, as if someone today invented a dial-up modem.

There are other endings to Le Prince's story. In 1966 a researcher into early cinema unearthed a note written by the director of the Dijon Municipal Library: *Le Prince est mort à Chicago en 1898, disparition volontaire exigée par la famille. Homosexualité.* As with so many aspects of the story, this explanation provokes more questions than it answers. Who was it written to, and why? What was Le Prince doing in Chicago? Why 'at the family's request'? And that last, terse word?

In 2003, a photograph of a drowned man resembling Le Prince, dated 1890, was found in Paris police archives. If it is Le Prince, the irony: to disappear, and then be discovered by a photo. We are undone by that which we do.

We have only the word of Le Prince's brother that he actually boarded the train at Dijon that day. No other witnesses came forward. From Dijon trains only headed northeast to Paris, and south to Marseilles. It is possible that Le Prince did indeed get on that train to Paris, then jumped, and headed south.

The train arriving in the Lumières' film moves so quickly it is easy to ignore everything else happening, the crowd pushed out of the way of advancing modernity. But look carefully: Thirty seconds in, someone leans from a window, readying himself to open the door as the train draws to a halt. A tall, thin man leaps out with an agility that belies his age. Even though he looks scarcely over thirty, he must be nearly fifty-five by now, his moustache shorter, befitting the fashion of the times. He has no luggage or bags of any kind. He hunches his shoulders in that way tall people have of trying to make themselves look shorter, less obtrusive. He's also thinner than the well-built athlete described by others. Perhaps he hasn't eaten well for the past few years. What has he been doing? Where has he been?

He steps out of the carriage and looks back questioningly, as if expecting another person to follow or be waiting on the platform, perhaps. Then someone bumps into him, he turns, notices the camera, and hastily shuffles out of the frame. He is on screen for less than five seconds.

I watch the film over and over again, its few seconds as tantalising as the *Roundhay Garden Scene*. There is no sound, of course, nothing more than a few seconds of image to give up their secrets.

No trains arrive in La Ciotat anymore. The station is abandoned, though it has not yet disappeared. An occasional TGV thunders through, too fast for a Lumière camera to capture anything other than a rapid black blur. Usurped by better, more famous stories and a voracious patent-grabber, Le Prince has been written out of history. And though you may watch that originary film again and again, it will not give up its secrets.

SELF-PORTRAIT
AS A DROWNED MAN

He's too long, too straight, and uncomfortably folded at the wrong angles. It looks like someone has bent him to fit the frame, post mortem. His head is propped against an indiscernible bulky object, as though this man has ended his days in a store cupboard. Two curls of black hair, their lacquer lasting beyond death, point to the centre of his forehead. There's a large circular object to his right, our left: a closer look shows it to be a straw sunhat. His face is slightly blackened, as if he's been beaten up, or asphyxiated, but the hands, too, are livid. It may be nothing more than sunburn—this man a bargeman or farm labourer come to the city, his face and hands exposed to the elements (redness could not be captured in such an early photograph, only a smudgy near-black). A drape falls across his knees, his hands folded upon it. A winding sheet, unwound.

· · ·

The corpse that you see before you is that of M. Bayard, inventor of the process whose marvellous results you are witnessing. To the best of

my knowledge, this ingenious man and indefatigable seeker had been
working to perfect his invention for almost three years.

The Academy, the King, and all those who have seen his im-
ages—which he found imperfect—have admired them as you ad-
mire them in this moment. This brought him great honour, and yet
he was not worth a quarter of a sou. The government, so generous
with M. Daguerre, said it could do nothing for M. Bayard, so the
unfortunate man drowned himself. Oh, the instability of all that
is human! Artists, experts, and newspapers so long occupied them-
selves with him, yet for several days now he has been lying on show
in the morgue, and no one has either recognised or claimed him. La-
dies and gentlemen, pass by for fear your sense of smell should be
offended: the man's face and hands are, as you can see, beginning to
rot. H.B., 18 October 1840.

This is all he wrote. His handwriting on the back of a photograph, later called *La Noyade*, one of the first ever made.

• • •

Arago always visits at night. Bayard hears the footsteps creaking on
the stairs, then glances out of his window to see the carriage below,
black horses impatiently waiting.

'Bonsoir, Monsieur. I welcome you.'

'Yes. Again.'

'I thank you for your interest. You must be such a busy man.'

'Oh, I am. I am. But something as important as this merits

my precious time.' Arago. Arrogant, thinks Bayard, this should be his name.

'I thank you again for your courtesy.' Bayard has worked as a clerk in the Ministry of Finance for nearly twenty years now and knows how to flatter, or if not to flatter, then at least how to address such a distinguished visitor correctly. He gestures to the armchair, the only one in the apartment, but Arago shakes his head.

'I'm always afraid of getting lost out here.' Bayard deflects what he thinks Arago intends as an insult.

'I am not a rich man, Monsieur. I dedicate my time to my work.' Bayard does not continue, does not want to plead penury. He feels no embarrassment about his lodgings.

'Of course.'

Arago, the visitor, is a heliographer: an expert of light. He has measured it, found its speed, its form as a wave, has used it to measure the circumference of the earth and investigate the magnetic effects of the aurora borealis. He is Director of the Observatory, Perpetual Secretary of the Academy of Sciences. Bayard knows what it means to have such a man here, now, in this dark, quiet place.

'What brings you this night?'

Bayard asks the question out of formality, knowing that he, too, is a man obsessed with light, and has found a fellow obsessive. His father has told him the story of how, as a small child, he once stood with his back to the sun and cast a shadow on the rough earth of their farmland, then scratched a line around his umbral presence in the dirt, bursting into tears when he returned to find an empty shape. Since then, Bayard has given his life to the attempt to hold light in his hand as if water. He soaked paper in red carthamin, the tincture gained from squeezing out the thorny plants that infested their land in late summer, then placed leaves and flowers on the wet sheets and watched their faint and discoloured images emerge then remain when left out in the sun. Later, he took a job with the inspectorate of taxes, earning just enough to finance his experiments, the purchase of silver chloride, alkaline iodides, little more. He has avidly followed the work of Daguerre and Niépce, subscribed to the journal of proceedings of the Académie des Beaux-Arts, and now invented a process he calls *heliography*.

'An Englishman, a certain Mr. Fox Talbot, is close to perfecting the process of fixing images on paper.'

'But I have already done so, Monsieur Arago. You know.'

A year has passed since Bayard made his first heliographs: the windmills in Montmartre; a deserted place de la Concorde; the dome of the Invalides. He had them exhibited, his newfangled wonder part of a charity show to raise money for victims of a recent earthquake in Martinique. The critic Francis Wey was so impressed with the images, he talked of setting up an institute of heliographers. 'They resembled nothing I had ever seen,' Wey wrote, 'They unite the impression of reality with the fantasy of dreams: light grazes and shadow caresses them.' Nothing had ever moved Bayard so much. He stood on a threshold, smelled success. This is why Arago sought him out.

The first time Arago visited they talked late into the night. Arago recounted tales of his visit to the extreme north and seeing the ghostly lights floating above its horizon, of founding the Observatory, of his travels around the Mediterranean to measure the meridian and discover the exact length of a metre, of his flight from a Spanish prison and his capture by corsairs. A showman, he talked of Algiers, of the months spent in the lazaretto wasting from a mysterious disease on his return, of addressing the Royal Society in London. And then, well onto their second candle, of magnetism, of sound waves, of light: its separation into distinct elements, its speed. Its beauty.

His second visit, they talked of heliography. Arago had enquired as to Bayard's methods and processes, the chemicals he used, his exposure times. Bayard sensed his inquisitor's enthusiasm, and warmed: this silent, single-minded man becoming more garrulous, vaunting his success.

'But Bayard, you are not alone—you have many competitors,' cut in Arago.

'No, Monsieur—this is not a competition, not a race.' He dared to correct the tall thin man, who remained, for a moment, wordless. 'We are all as men scrabbling around in a darkened room, with nothing but a single taper each,' he continued. 'Were we to put our faint torches together—we could start a fire!' Arago seemed not to understand.

'Monsieur Daguerre is close to perfecting his process.' Bayard was intrigued, though he knew from what he had read that Daguerre's technique was very different from his own.

'We should share our knowledge, Monsieur Arago. In the interests of science, of progress, of heliography!' Arago took his stick and left without even shaking his head.

Tonight is different. Bayard senses his visitor's anxiety, the desire to settle his business hurriedly.

'Time presses, Monsieur.' Arago opens his gloved hand, then squeezes an invisible object in its palm, as though he could hold time itself.

Bayard sits in the chair and allows himself to realise how much he hates the man as he at once wishes to impress him. Why should he offer his hospitality, meagre as it is, to this interloper, this broker of power and influence? This is the third time he has come now, and Bayard will silver his tongue with the courteous forms their respective positions require no longer. Everything he has achieved, he has achieved alone. His genius should be recognised. Yet he wants no part in Arago's games, refuses to participate in deceit and manipulation.

Silence sits between them until Arago breaks it.

'Money is available.'

'Money is as nothing to the recognition I deserve,' snaps Bayard.

'Recognition, Monsieur Bayard, as you call it, is an ephemeral thing, and arbitrarily given. A small sum of money, I am sure, would help you far much more than having some people in the Academy chattering about you. Had I been interested only in recognition, Sir,

I would have achieved nothing. Dedication to the ideal is what is necessary.' He looks around the apartment. 'Some money may help you.' He is not wrong, Bayard knows, and feels his nose unwillingly hooked. Arago will make a great politician, realises Bayard.

'What kind of a sum is being mentioned?'

'Six hundred francs.'

'Six hundred? But Monsieur Daguerre has secured ten thousand.'

'Six hundred. That is the most we can offer. For a man from, well, such a station as yourself, I'm sure this will be most welcome.' Six hundred francs. Coins on his eyes, nothing more.

What will six hundred francs buy? Time, and materials. It is something.

'I assume that in exchange for the sum I will be expected to contribute to the Academy's proceedings.' They are trying to buy his genius, thinks Bayard without rancour. He is prepared to share his knowledge.

'No, Monsieur. That will not be necessary.' It is worse: they are not trying to buy his secrets, but his silence.

His night visitor has come and offered him a deal. Then so be it. He will accept the money. Let Arago ferry him across the river.

• • •

In the time the Seine still froze, the spring thaw brought a harvest of bodies. Between April 1795 and September 1801, 306 bodies were taken from the river and temporarily placed in a morgue. The morgue's two attendants, Bouille and Daude, recorded them all, methodically noting the full particulars of each corpse: sex, age, hair colour, the bodily wounds and scars. If the body was clothed, a full description of the cut, colour, and condition of the clothing was registered, as well as any contents of the pockets. Not all of their subjects would have drowned: the river also drew those who perished by accident, misadventure, murder, or suicide.

Bouille and Daude's records end at the beginning of the nineteenth century; we do not know why. They may have moved on, passed away themselves, or simply tired of their exhaustive and seemingly pointless cataloguing. Even had they still been working as late as 1840, however, they wouldn't have found the corpse of Hippolyte Bayard.

. . .

Announcing a truth involves the stipulation of an enigma: Roland Barthes's lapidary description of the outset of Poe's 'The Facts in the Case of M. Valdemar,' the tale of a man mesmerised while dying, enabling him to speak from beyond death. Poe had his story published anonymously, its anonymity posing as a claim to truth. It's difficult to know how many people believed the ruse, as claims to truth were common in such fiction at the time.

Bayard may have read the tale, in Baudelaire's translation. His own story was similar: Bayard, too, announced his truth—the photograph, its message on the reverse—yet in so doing stipulated more than one enigma.

The truth he announced was that of the photograph: a simultaneous reality and fiction. Hippolyte Bayard never drowned himself. The photograph is a fake.

• • •

He undresses, throwing his clothes onto the armchair, then wraps a bedsheet around himself and sits on the pile of fruit boxes he has dragged in from the street. No, the sheet is too high: his face must be clearly visible. They must know who they are dealing with. He pulls the sheet down, uncovering his torso, feels cold air on his skin, and wonders what it will be like to be dead. The morgue would have given him answers, but he has flinched from the idea of visiting. He imagines stiffness, the rigour of new death. He blackens his face and hands with the burnt cork of a wine bottle to mimic decomposition.

Each exposure will take twelve minutes. He closes his eyes and waits while his lens watches him. It's cold in his room. Even live sitters have to close their eyes: if eyes move during the exposure, they disappear. He worries it will be too dark to make two further exposures should the first fail.

• • •

Disgusted by the way he had been treated by future prime minister François Arago, possibly jealous of Daguerre's brief but phenomenal success, Bayard left Paris in the early 1840s for the quiet provincial town of Nemours, where he lived until he was eighty. He worked on his heliographs, with some small success. He never seems to have married. Little more is known about him.

• • •

Why fake a suicide? Pathological morbid obsessions, psychological disorders. A cry for help is the obvious answer, the desperate bid for attention. Neither of these explain Bayard's action: Bayard faked his suicide as a protest. Yet the walls of the Academy remained unbreached and Arago became a yet greater man; Bayard was largely forgotten and his work left unrecognised. The effects of a photograph, however, are not easy to predict: Who can say what Bayard's self-portrait achieved, who saw it, who it haunted?

One of the first photographs; the first photographic fake. Truth upstaged. The reception of the photograph and its grim text is not recorded, yet it seems improbable that anyone would have taken it seriously. The disingenuousness of the message 'to the best of my knowledge'—of course he knew. Signing it off with his own initials, while simultaneously claiming to be dead. Is this a message from beyond death, mesmerically delivered, perhaps, in the style of Poe's M. Valdemar? Or is it that a photograph itself has the power to speak from beyond? The initials simultaneously claim authorship, truth, and authority, while attesting the death of its author. Or perhaps it was just a joke.

Why did Bayard decide on drowning? Why did he not hang himself, or portray himself languishing, Chatterton-like, a half-full bottle of poison in hand? A gunshot or stab wound would obviously have been more difficult to fake. Throwing oneself under a train was becoming an increasingly popular method: had Bayard been born later, he might have chosen the network of lines and escapes the railway provided to disappear into, but his century was still mapped by the river. In thrall to the magic of light, Bayard was still of alchemy as much as science.

• • •

Much later, he watches the thick grass in the overgrown garden fading in the late summer sun. He looks at his hands and notes how the sun has left its mark on them, too. Liver spots fleck his loose skin as if foxed paper. His own body is a photograph, his own skin dyed by his own hand and left in the light to record an image.

What image would it store, what story could his body tell?

That of the Mission Heliographique he finally managed to establish, the six-month journey out into the remains of rural France, the collection of heliographs: collapsing barns, abandoned farm buildings, rotting barges. Things captured the moment before they disappeared forever.

Or that of his invention of combination printing. Putting two negatives together to achieve an image that could capture the most evanescent of things: clouds in motion, the flight of a bird, the flicker of a sitter's eyes. They'd criticised this, too. He had given the camera the ability to lie.

Things missing. That is what his body would record: his photograph, his absence. His earliest pictures are fading now, and will soon disappear altogether, leaving nothing but faintly stained paper.

He feels the sun burning him despite the late hour and moves to go inside. His joints ache as he stands, reminding him that he is a body, not an image, after all.

To be this, here, now. To exist, even if no one should ever know, does that amount to something? Photography is a way of creating permanence where none exists. He knows what will survive him, what will remain: an image of his dead body. Hippolyte Bayard has cheated death with an image of himself as a dead man.

EVERYTHING IS SUBJECT TO MOTION, AND EVERYTHING IS MOTION'S SUBJECT

While the other children gather in the schoolyard, Étienne-Jules Marey goes searching for frogs.

Shame, that to measure the beat of the frog's heart they have to stop it. His schoolteacher, underqualified but eager to help this curious boy, shows no remorse: 'It has no soul,' he says.

With doll's limbs, cogs from a broken clock, and thread from the sewing box, Étienne-Jules fashions a mechanical animal, which will not stop when he shows his sisters how it works. They laugh at the strange thing hopping round on the carpet, amazed, delighted, disturbed.

• • •

It takes one tenth of a second, he learns, for a sensory impulse to reach the brain. He sticks a pin into his finger.

How fast does thought travel? he wonders, noting the ruby of blood on his copybook. He watches it congeal. Faster than that, he thinks.

A beam of sun lights motes of chalk dust in the heavy afternoon air. Names scratched into the wooden desks become bas-reliefs, traces of an ancient civilisation. The lecture bores him. He's better than this already. *Summa cum laude* awaits, but he has a question: 'We can measure the pulse, the breath, the articulation of the joints, the speed of a running man, but what links them?'

'Perhaps you should study philosophy, maître, and not physiology.'

. . .

Her husband runs a newspaper. They come to his public lectures. Marey writes an article for the *Globe*, visits M. Vilbort's office, then the printers, watches the presses grinding, whirring, and running endlessly, spitting out sheet after sheet after sheet. Time compressed into their pages.

Madame Vilbort is unwell, will move south. Monsieur will remain in Paris: the paper, of course.

But that mole on the side of her neck, the curve of her earlobe, the flutter of her fingers as she lifts her hands to explain what she means. *Oh*, there are no words.

. . .

There is no discrete moment, nothing is separated from anything else. Everything overlaps. Love too. He needs a discreet moment.

He spends too much time in libraries and research institutes, talking to dull men and reading duller books. The laboratory is better.

The world cannot be grasped by merely looking. He needs to understand flow, turbulence, dynamics. Multiple images, he finds, can be recorded on a single plate. Motion and its image. Time passes across his pictures.

While others are busy with the transit of Venus, only tiny things interest him. He will occupy himself with the transit of a bird's wing, the fall of its feather, the movement of a fish's supple spine.

• • •

'Put a string of images,' he tells her over dinner, 'at least ten a second, across the viewer's eye and they will perceive movement through time and space.' She smiles and puts her glass down, encouraging him to continue. He wants to say more but cannot find the words and worries he is boring her. It is hot here in Naples, even at night, and the heat tires them. Sound too, he wants to say: there is no sound that takes less than a tenth of a second to say.

His photographs, he writes in letters back to Paris, are 'a natural expression that is not that of ordinary language: the latter is too slow and too imprecise to describe clearly, with their complexity and variability, the different acts of life.'

• • •

Gun over his shoulder, he walks the narrow path down the hill. At the bottom, there is a turn where it opens out to the bay. The fishermen eye him strangely. He soaks his shoes clambering over the rocks until he is as far out as possible, then waits until a gull in flight passes. He raises the gun, takes sight, and pulls the trigger, but there is no bang, no smoke from the barrel, and nothing falls from the sky. Marey turns to the fishermen and smiles; he has what he wants: the ballet of a bird's wings in flight.

'O scemo! laughs the boy, running after Marey as he heads back up the hill. The barefoot urchin points to make it clear who he's talking about, his mouth wide with an idiotic tongue-lolling grin. *Guarda! 'O scemo di Posillipo! 'O matto francese!* Look! The Posillipo idiot! The mad Frenchman! Marey has heard it before, is used to it. He turns, points the gun at the boy, and pulls the trigger.

The boy is scared a second, then realises nothing has happened, so continues with his taunting, not knowing his image will still be seen more than a century later.

He has had the barrel of the gun fashioned specially for him, then mounted on an old stock. A camera instead of a lock. It shoots twelve frames per second, the chronophotographic gun.

The clock, the phonograph, and the camera fix time. Chronophotography tries to escape it.

• • •

As she lies asleep, he watches the slow rise and fall of her chest, notes the scarcely perceptible pulse at her wrists, senses the breath that passes between her lips. He is as passionate as a scientist and as cold as a lover.

If this moment, too, could be out of time, if it could be endless circulation and flow. No motion other than that of the heart.

In life, this tangle. His constant passage from Paris to Naples, Naples to Paris. The demands of work, love, money pushing him one way and pulling him the other. A life always in transition, never stopping, always moving. Always in the present tense. Were he to stop and think of the past or the future, what would happen? When and where, he sometimes thinks, will I finally rest? His life like his pictures: tracing a motion back and forth across Europe.

He should examine his heart. What keeps him like this, in an eternal affair with a woman married to someone else? If he examines his heart, he will have to stop it.

• • •

He takes the boat out with Dohrn. It is a day so perfect he hardly believes in it. Vesuvius squats to their left, Capri reclines on the horizon. The sky so blue it looks artificial. Dohrn: his only friend here in the city, another exile (though for science, not love). They watch the coil of smoke hanging above the volcano, the waves chopping at the side of the boat. The zoologist tells Marey about the fish-crowded sea. Gilt-head bream, sea bass, red mullet, moray eel leap to the surface, eager to be observed. 'And here,' says Dohrn, scooping ectoplasm from the water, '*Olindias phosphorica*, a luminous jellyfish. The locals call them "medusas."'

Marey has his gun with him and makes everything still. The moment can't be captured, but its impossibility can.

• • •

He can time a heartbeat, picture the folding of a wing in flight, and weigh the pressure of air on a falling feather. His question now: How can you observe what is invisible?

He is dubious about the limits of human perception and sometimes wishes he were a machine, his gun an extension of his arm, a part of him. He wants to trace everything and record those traces without interference. He wants nature to write itself.

There is no memory in his work: it has to be the moment itself, freed from the weight of the past and the present and the future.

He shows Madame his latest work, how he has photographed a spark. 'It looks like a snowflake,' she says. 'A river, the branches of a tree, the human nervous system.'

• • •

He moves, things move around him, yet everything stays the same. His life ends in Naples or Paris or somewhere between the two, passing out of the edge of the frame. He becomes a progenitor, an influencer, an experimenter and inventor, never the thing he was. His name moves through footnotes, obscure essays, and elliptical poems, lives on in archives.

His last photographs are nothing but smoke. They look like spirit photographs, pneuma, a breath before it stops.

Echoes and repetitions, patterns and endless form most beautiful. This is what he finds. And what he desires: not the bird he has photographed but the air around it, not the fish but the water it swims through.

I'M IN LOVE WITH
A GERMAN FILM STAR

THE PASSIONS–'I'M IN LOVE WITH
A GERMAN FILM STAR' (POLYDOR 7", 1981)

Four slow notes of shiver, blush, echoplex, and delay, then a tiny cascade, a shimmer, and a drop. A perfectly distracted rhythm section. A cold glow of voice. Not the first record I ever bought, but the first time I ever *heard* music.

It's a glamorous world. It hadn't been, but now it was.

THE CURE–'ALL CATS ARE GREY'
(FROM *FAITH*, FICTION, 1981)

I lay on the threadbare carpet in my room and watched the lights from passing cars throw abstract movies across the walls. I'd put this on and the room became a cathedral of shadow and smoke. It's the last track on side one and the tone arm on my record player didn't work properly so the music faded into the hiss and scratch of the run-out groove. Even then, I knew that somewhere out there, Magda was listening to this, too.

LA DÜSSELDORF–'SILVER CLOUD'
(TELDEC 7", 1976)

I wouldn't hear this until much later, but when I did I knew that Magda had spent the long summer of 1976 dancing to it with a boy called Andreas or Jürgen or Max who was not worthy of her.

BERNTHØLER–'MY SUITOR'
(BLANCO Y NEGRO 7", 1984)

A video shop had opened between the chippy and the florist and as if by accident or magic they had a small section of the titles I only ever saw namechecked in the NME or showing at the Aaben in Hulme. The owner didn't seem to know what certificate they were and didn't blink when I checked out *Herzen und Knochen*. It isn't her best film, but it was enough.

Magda's luminous face appears fifteen minutes in. Her first word—*zwischen*—is a mere preposition that becomes a jouissant epiphany as she says it. All my future lay in those five phonemes.

John Peel played this record around the same time, but I couldn't get hold of it until it received a UK release nearly a year later. For some reason I became convinced that Magda was the singer, even though I knew it wasn't her. I could hear her, I thought, singing to me through it. The last scene of the film would have been so much better had this been its soundtrack.

THE DURUTTI COLUMN–'SKETCH FOR DAWN (II)'
(FROM *LC*, FACTORY, 1982)

An example of how music can go beyond evocation to become the thing itself. The bass is a long narrow avenue somewhere in Europe, the piano the high windows of a slightly shabby late-nineteenth-century apartment building, its echo the footsteps in their stairwells. There are trees, it is late summer or early autumn. The guitar is the touch of mist in the air.

Vini Reilly (who *is* the Durutti Column) recorded this in a damp flat in Chorlton, but several years later I would find myself buying then living in the place he had brought into being in this song, on the street that had been one of the principal locations for *Die Flammende Haut.*

Dreams burnt away / by the first cigarette of the day. I'm not sure if it was this line or the way Magda held a cigarette in *Herzen und Knochen* that made me take up smoking. I blame neither of them for it.

ASSOCIATES–'WHITE CAR IN GERMANY'
(SITUATION TWO 12", 1981)

I'm listing the twelve-inch here, but it is also track one, side one of the duo's *Fourth Drawer Down* LP, which I listened to obsessively on a Walkman throughout 1982 as I took the bus to school, already seeing myself on the open autobahn, speeding past cities, through forests, and over bridges in a vintage Porsche 911 convertible, a scene that would form the title sequence of *Tränen sind im Regen unsicht-bar*, Magda's only venture into romantic comedy, and still much underappreciated.

WIM MERTENS–'STRUGGLE FOR PLEASURE' (ARIOLA/LES DISQUES DU CRÉPESCULE 12", 1983)

It's been used everywhere (phone adverts, a Peter Greenaway film, some god-awful Café del Mar chill-out compilation) and at first I thought I'd leave it out, but I'm certain I remember hearing it over the tannoy in Brussel-Zuid, or perhaps it was Köln Hauptbahnhof, or maybe Amsterdam Centraal, that first time I boarded a train to the Continent. On one long leg of the journey I met a girl called Claudia, who was interested in me because I was pretending to read Kafka, and who I was interested in because I told myself she looked like Magda. She fell asleep on my shoulder and woke up when we got to Hannover, or Hamburg, or somewhere, then got off, leaving me her name and address written on a slip of paper that I put between the leaves of the Penguin Modern Classic and forgot about, until now, when I listen to this piece of music again.

ROBERT GÖRL–'MIT DIR' (MUTE 12", 1983)

Find the video for this and at three minutes forty seconds in, watch very carefully to see Magda appear as one of the faces in the slowly dancing crowd. The camera closes in on her and then, as if almost afraid of so much beauty, rapidly cuts away.

GRAUZONE–'EISBÄR' (EMI ELECTROLA 7", 1981)

In a small feature in *Kino* magazine (Sept '83), Magda lists this as one of her favourite records.

CLOCK DVA–'FOUR HOURS' (FETISH 7", 1981)

Many years later I got a rare chance to see *Mein Herz ist eine Bombe, mein Kopf ist ein Gedicht* while sitting on an upturned beer crate in a Kreuzberg basement. An experimental short made while Magda was still a drama student, it's not part of her official filmography (as much as one exists at all), but essential viewing for anyone seriously interested.

As the Super 8 projector spooled and whirred and the image on the screen flickered, I knew that the director of the film and Magda had been fucking while listening to this record.

NEU–'SEELAND'
(FROM *NEU 75*, UNITED ARTISTS, 1975)

This is the music in the closing scenes of *Die Flammende Haut,* where we see Magda walking for hours through the deserted city, alone, as dawn slowly breaks and she eventually reaches the sea. I knew the song long before I got to see the film and when I saw it, it felt like a homecoming. There is no more poignant scene in the history of cinema.

The film is currently unavailable on streaming, DVD, or even VHS, so I have instead played my copy of the record so often I can no longer tell where the rain effect ends and the surface noise of the worn vinyl begins.

DAVID BOWIE–'HELDEN' (RCA 7", 1977)

Via the address of the production company listed at the end of *Haut*, I wrote to Magda asking what this song meant to her, or even—I hoped!—if she would record herself singing it. I never received a reply, and suspect that this is because while Bowie himself remained tight-lipped on the subject, the two must have run into each other during his time in Berlin. The much-discussed line *and we kissed / as though nothing could fall* can only refer to Magda. His decision to record this version of his most bleakly yearning and melancholically ecstatic song *auf Deutsch* was surely an indirect message to her.

BLONDIE–'ATOMIC' (CHRYSALIS 7", 1980)

Silbernes Feuer, Magda's last film, was famously troubled. On-set tensions, three directors, and a production company going bust meant it was never properly finished, and despite the existence of several dubious 'final' cuts it has never received an official release. This song was supposed to accompany the climactic scene in which Magda leads revellers from a nightclub onto the streets of a collapsing city, but licensing issues rendered it unavailable. It was replaced with a cover version by legendary DDR punk band Zwitschermaschine, which I have sadly been unable to track down.

TONNETZ–'MAGDA' (CHAIN REACTION 12", 1997)

All glitch and sparkle, this immersive piece of low-slung minimal techno I found via a recommendation on a discussion board dedicated to German cinema. The site told me many things: that she had married four times; that she was living in Los Angeles and working on a new film; that she had undergone extensive cosmetic surgery in order never to be recognised again; that she still loved clubbing; that she had been a Stasi agent; that 'Magda' was only ever a pseudonym used to cover her real identity; that she had made several other films that had gone straight to streaming; that she was living in Prestwich; that she had never really existed at all. I knew most of these theories were nonsense.

ALVA NOTO–'A FOREST' (NOTON DL, 2020)

The famous Cure song stripped to vapour traces, murmurs, and distant sighs. This was playing out in Berghain when I saw her again. Despite the darkness I recognised her immediately but did not approach as I had been taking some very strong painkillers while recovering from the high-speed accident that had written off the Porsche. She was dancing, of course, incredibly slowly, alone, and unselfconscious. I wanted to leave her that way.

This is the only Magda song that I do not possess as an object (its only physical form is an extremely expensive limited edition etched disc that I can no longer afford), and I rue this absence, as I fear my memories and dreams will vanish as quickly as a single spoken word or the vision of a face on a screen if I cannot touch them.

VIOLINS AND PIANOS ARE HORSES

As the Composer returned, toward the end of what he suspected but did not yet know would be the end of his life, to a town that sat on an elbow of the Danube, where as a child he had heard the Turkish of the Turks, the demotic of the Greeks, the Ladino of the Sephardic Jews, and the German of anyone who'd travelled north and considered themselves a rung up on the social ladder, a town made up of the way it spoke and how it sounded, a town of Circassians, Albanians, Armenians, Romanians from across the river, and Russians from the other side of the Black Sea, a rusty old river port where timber was shipped out and grain picked up, a traveller's rest on the route to Sofia or Vienna or Varna, the first thing that struck him was the sight of a working horse.

The Composer's daughter offered him her arm as they climbed out of the taxi that had brought them from the station to the Hotel Plaza, and together they were splashed by the muddy water from a puddle disturbed by the hooves and spindly legs of a small horse, more a pony, half donkey, which pulled a rickety trap run by an old man who looked like the old men the Composer remembered from his boyhood. Had they always been here, he thought, was there an endless supply of such men? Next to him sat a boy, his son or grandson, wearing a tired pink nylon shirt, not different from the youths the Composer had seen on streets in Paris, London, and New York. The old man casually lengthened his arm and struck the animal across its flank with a long black stick, and it broke from a hobble into a lame trot.

With one arm linked around his daughter's and the other clutching his own stick, the Composer limped into the foyer of the hotel, where they were greeted by soft lights and anonymous music, as though they had crossed a threshold back into a world more familiar to them. They changed, then took dinner together in the restaurant, where he chose the kavarma, and they sat in a near silence broken only by Irene's warnings about cholesterol. He could not finish the dish but would not give up, and Irene distracted him by asking questions, wanting to know how he felt, what he remembered, what it was like to return, but the Composer brushed off her inquiries, irritated not only by the American twang of her voice, the upward swing of her affirmative sentences, questioning and vulnerable, but also, he knew, because he had no answers for her. He hardly recognised the place he had returned to as the one where he had been born.

The sight of the suffering beast on the road was still disturbing him, like the heartburn he could already feel. For a distracted moment he had been tempted to throw his arms round the horse and weep, filled with admiration and pity for its depleted strength, for its insistence, for its courage, for its blunt hope. He chided himself for being sentimental, but the uneasy compassion that filled him provoked a memory of his experiments with pianos, of how he had opened the coffin-like body with the reverence of a surgeon or a priest, seen the thing's sinews and bones laid out before him, placed stones or coins on the metal strings to temper their sound. Is this how the horse would end up, too? Poked and prodded by strangers, its hair used to make blankets, its flesh used to feed the poor, its bones boiled down for glue?

The Composer knew full well where the horse would finish up when the boy or his father or someone else saw the animal finally refuse to move any farther, just as the Roma who had come past their house every Friday when he was a child had known. Irene was baffled but remained silent, used to her father's strange tangents, when the Composer began to tell her the stories of how fascinated and frightened he had been by the Roma, how he'd heard they came from India or somewhere farther east in the times before Alexander the Great, how he'd heard they brought good luck, or bad luck, or stole children, and so was careful to watch them from the safety of the window when they passed, and the maid took food out for them while they sat cross-legged on the dirty floor of the yard and smoked and played music on ragged violins with scarves tied around their necks, punctured lung accordions, and a ruptured drum.

The Composer said good night to his daughter and went up to bed, leaving Irene alone in the bar. Before he fell into a fitful sleep he thought of how she had been stolen from him, not by Roma, but by schools in Paris, clothes shopping in London, by Ohio, her home now. His life could mean nothing to her.

That night he dreamed of the horse. He was a child again, out walking with his father through the streets of the town he remembered, though now lined by huge windowless hotels. The land around lay flat, silent and lifeless but garishly illuminated by theatre lights. The same trap passed them and splashed them again, and a group of villagers with poorly drawn, unfinished faces gathered round them to laugh. The driver took out his stick and began to beat the horse as if punishing it for its misdemeanour, until the creature's swollen belly became a drum keeping some brutal rhythm. The half-faced people began to sing in time with the rhythm, a wordless, howling song that grew faster and faster until words started to form. They were willing the horse back up again, trying to make it walk one last stretch, as far as the knacker's yard. He asked his father to make the Friday violinist come and play, hoping his music would be enough to make the horse rise, heal, and walk again, then dance, then fly, and take the violinist flying after him.

Next morning the Composer woke feeling feverish and wondered if he was starting to fall ill. How would Irene manage if he were to be taken sick here? She had none of the languages. The hospitals were probably terrible. He remembered his mother coping with five children after his father had dropped suddenly dead one day, aged forty, less than half his age now. He had become father to his young brothers until, aged nineteen, he had left for Vienna to study music, encouraged so much to do so by his mother, who had then spent the rest of her life blaming him for having deserted her.

At breakfast he found Irene already seated at their table and laughing far too loudly with the waiter who had also been the barman the evening before. She introduced her father to Sorin, who in turn greeted the Composer in English. Sorin offered to take them around the town, but the Composer declined, in Bulgarian, telling the boy that he already knew the place, even as they both knew this to be a lie.

They set out on foot with no destination other than the vague aim of finding the Composer's childhood home. I want you to see it, he told Irene, so you can meet the grandmother you never had. They got lost on a busy road somewhere outside the Metro superstore and argued until Irene found the way back to the town centre and they ended up in a park where the Composer thought he had played with a hobbyhorse. The memory was like a smell, waking things he'd thought forgotten before they'd even been remembered. The hobbyhorse loomed in his mind with disturbing clarity. It had been a present from an uncle in England, he remembered, who had later drowned at sea.

They walked along a street whose name he recognised, though all the buildings were unfamiliar until he found the house in which he believed he had been born. In his pocket he carried the key that his mother had given him when he left, telling him he would always be welcome to return, whenever he needed. Irene pushed a button on the intercom and a voice, all incomprehension and crackle, asked who they were. The Composer had kept the key for sixty-seven years, but only now realised it would no longer work.

A short, stout woman wearing a worn blue apron came to the door and told them the house had long been divided into flats and that she couldn't possibly let them in. They heard the sound of a television blaring and some children fighting within. This place was only built fifty, maybe sixty years ago anyhow, said the woman, it can't possibly be the place you're looking for. The Composer and Irene looked at each other and said nothing, and the woman shut the door on them without saying goodbye.

They walked away, with no direction, arm in arm like a five-legged creature, the Composer's black walking stick their extra appendage. He had hoped, if not expected, that someone would have recognised him, or known his name, or his family's name. He had hoped, against hope, to find someone to welcome him, to ask after his mother, his brothers, his sisters. They have taken away my memory, he thought.

He wanted to go back to the house and tell the slatternly looking mother that he, the Composer, had an entry in the *Grove Dictionary of Music*, he wanted to tell her that he could have studied with Schoenberg, and about his time at Darmstadt, and his arguments with Stockhausen and being invited to Paris for a residency at Ircam. He wanted to tell them that he, the Composer, had seen seasons dedicated to his music in halls almost filled with earnest audiences from

Tokyo to Stockholm to Seattle, that a conference in Cincinnati had been held in his honour. He wanted to talk to her, or anyone, about serialism, and post-serialism, about atonality or the wisdom of appropriating folk melodies. He did not want to tell anyone that none of his work had been performed for over a decade now, nor that it was no longer studied in any Conservatory he knew of, nor that he had been accused of being both willfully difficult and sentimentally populist. He did not want anyone to remind him of the fool who had written on his Wikipedia page that his early promise had ultimately led nowhere.

Nowhere? Here? Back to a town he could no longer recognise?

They found themselves back at the grubby junction outside the Metro superstore, unable to cross the busy road.

'This place is a fucking dump,' said Irene.

Irene did not want to spend another evening in the hotel, so later that afternoon they went out again to find a café Sorin the barman had recommended. Recorded music played at a volume that made the Composer feel ill, and the lighting was sure to bring on a migraine. He wanted to sit outside, but Irene told him it was too cold. He was, at least, pleased to see a few men as old as himself there, a few sitting alone, others in small groups, and realised he may have known them as children, perhaps gone to school with them, though he recognised no one. Irene was the only woman there. After some time the Composer realised what the music was: an old Romanian song, but sung by a squealing child with an unceasing electronic thud behind it. He was pleased when it stopped and the boy from the cart with the grubby pink shirt reappeared with a group of men—some almost as old as the Composer, others young enough to be their sons or grandsons—all carrying instruments: a violin, an accordion, a double bass, a cimbalom, and a trumpet, which struck even the Composer as an unusual ensemble. They started to play, and after several false starts, one instrument tentatively picking out a melody or rhythm before realising the others weren't keeping up, they stopped and began to argue. The player of the double bass propped his instrument against the wall and went to the bar. They weren't listening to each other, thought the Composer.

A fresh round of drinks bought, they began again, but fell apart again after only a few bars. They were hopelessly out of time. They were more interested in drinking than playing. They argued again, now openly shouting at one another. The oldest man scowled at the youngest, who was impatient to play as fast as possible. The bass player began again with a forlorn limp and lope, counterpointing the arguing voices. One by one, the others ceased talking and joined in, the sound gradually gaining force above the smoke and chatter of the bar. This time it didn't fall apart. The Composer recognised this tune too, an old one they had used to make bears dance. Even as it stayed together and slowly grew, he disliked it. It reminded him too acutely of the cruelty of shows he had seen as a child and how they had upset him, but it continued to build, to spread, to grow, faster now. Yes, he remembered this piece, this is how it went, the slow start, then the increasing tempo. The musicians' hands and fingers moved in rhythm, sequence, harmony. Faster, then faster, then faster. Not only tempo but volume. Louder, then louder, then louder. All bar chatter ceased or was drowned. The hands and fingers of the players became a blur. It was too fast, too loud, too much. The bar standers whooped, yelled, clapped. The Composer hated its cheap sentimentality, the banal melody, the flashy technique of the players, the speed and volume with no nuance. And then the bass hicked up, split, as though there were two instruments or the player had four hands. Feet stamped. The music slipped into a time signature even the Composer did not recognise. The squawking trumpet shattered and played overtones, as if its player sounded both the instrument and its echo. The fiddler was deranged, surely. This was rough music, dirt music, music with one leg, a song their grandfathers had taught them and that their grandfathers had been taught by the Lord, or whoever they worshipped, the song their grandmothers wept to as they were bartered into marriage or they buried their dead children. The cimbalom opened its bass and built and boomed like the thunder of divine judgement. The volume, impossibly, continued to rise. Everyone in the café beat on tables, singing wordlessly, howling, stamping, shouting, no longer accompanying but all participating, creating the song, the sound, the music. The players, both wild-eyed and blank staring, were lost: they had become deliverers, messengers, vessels for a sound that came from they knew not where. There was sweat in their hair, blood in their eyes, and madness on their fingers. They were playing so they could fly, so they could leave this place, so they could bring dead horses back to life. They no longer played the music, it was playing them.

And then it stopped.

A string had been broken, a finger bled, the trumpeter could no longer stand. Nothing but a brief echo escaped like smoke through the door. One man, only, clapped; the others looked almost ashamed, as if waking from a drunken bender. The musicians, winded, fallen, collected their things and began to slope off. The Composer and his daughter threw them a US dollar, knowing how pathetic it was.

On the second night of his attempt to find home, the Composer lay on his hotel bed and tried to fall asleep but failed due to a persistent buzzing in his ears, the effect, he hoped, of having mixed the gritty red wine he had drunk in the bar with the pills he had to take for his heart, though he feared it was the musicians' nemesis, the bells, the one thing all members of his profession dreaded, the audiological malady he would not even name to himself in the private intimacy of near sleep, Beethoven's alleged end though he knew Beethoven hadn't really been thus afflicted but had beat his head against his piano after sawing off its legs because he was not able to express the symphony he could hear in his head because the instruments to make it had not yet been created, and with this thought he finally fell once again into fitful sleep to dream of music.

That night the Composer didn't dream images but sounds, a choir rising from the buzz in his ears to sing Renaissance polyphony in spherical, celestial, perfect harmony. The voices met and rose to the heavens, but the higher they ascended they began to fail, to break, and to rasp and buzz. Strange harmonies interrupted, the time signature changed, and the voices took on the sounds of the choirs of old women in the hills, moving easterly, southerly, until they became a muezzin's chant. Nothing he had ever heard, he thought lucidly during the dream, was as beautiful and as unharnessable as this sound. The music ebbed until he could hear only the babbling tongues of his childhood slowly merging with the rushing and burbling water of the river, until all was silence.

The next morning he went down to breakfast and found himself alone at their table. A polite waitress told him that Miss Irene hadn't come down yet. He looked for the boy Sorin, but he wasn't there either. The girl reminded him of someone, though he could not think who.

After breakfast he sat in the lobby reading newspapers he found incomprehensible, despite understanding all the words. He thought of going to wake his daughter but knew better. She eventually appeared around midday, looking ruffled, and told him he should have gone out for a walk and that it would do no good to sit around waiting for her.

He remembered who the waitress reminded him of. A cellist

he'd taught years ago in Paris. She had come to a master class he had given in his tall-windowed, white-walled apartment and stayed after the other students had gone. He had asked her to play for him. He remembered her face perfectly now, despite having forgotten it for so many years, but even though her dark-skinned, heavy-eyebrowed features were so clear, he could find no trace of her name in his memory, nor where she was from. Her arm had tensed as it held the bow across the strings, and she paused for the tiniest moment before taking a sudden sharp breath and beginning to play. He remembered seeing the hair under her armpit (a red dress, he remembered now, she was wearing a red sleeveless dress, it was hot, summer) and the thin line of sweat that formed on her upper lip as she bit down in concentration, her eyebrows touching in the middle as she wrinkled her forehead with the attack of the first note, the muscle taut beneath her brown skin, flexing as she held the neck of her instrument down, firmly, tightly, and used her bow to caress it with a mix of tenderness and violence, her face unbroken, a blank mask flashing into a split second of expression as the note went up, her lips parting, teeth visible, biting, and the sound of the amber body of the cello itself, sawing, buzzing, her eyes closed now, her arm moving faster and faster up the neck, her movements shorter, quicker, more precise as the sound became shorter, harder, sharper.

She stopped and looked surprised to find herself where she was. She had given herself up to let her hands be guided by her memory and her senses to bring forth sound from a piece of hollow wood and a few taut strings. It had been the grain of it, he thought, her body in the voice of the music, the points where the sound tensed and broke and twisted like a river breaking its banks, like a horse losing its reins, oblivious of what was creating it, that had made it unique. This was the music he should have written, though never did, this music could not be written, this music that he could only now capture through memory or dream.

Even though the Composer would be remembered after his death with retrospectives in Munich, London, and New York, the ragged café ensemble had a future playing in bars in Black Sea resorts and tube stations in Sofia, Athens, Naples, Rome, Paris, London. Their highlight would be the call to do a prestigious showcase event in a Berlin theatre that was self-sabotaged at their warm-up gig at a small club the evening before that ended with the accordion player getting violently drunk and swinging out at the violinist, who had meantime tried to make off with the evening's bar takings before getting belted by a baseball bat that the barman kept stashed for just such occasions. But it didn't matter because they knew, like the Composer now knew, that violins and pianos are the bodies of hardwood animals, their ringing tones empty ribcages with horsehair hobbyhorse manes dragged across horse head strings by nomads from central Asia, strength and sweetness and mystery for those who can't ride a violin or play the horse, music to make horses dance, to make them move, to bring forth the sweetness from the strength of the animal, the tethered recalcitrance of taut scraping strings, the hollow ribcage of the four-legged piano, horse-shaped as the violin is horse-headed, a scarf tied round its neck. The sound kicks up dust as it crosses the plains and charges into Europe to hold Vienna by siege before being let in and tamed by expert riders at the Spanish school, stolen from its smelly, thieving, unruly owners, cleaned and polished and painted and introduced into royal courts, then noble palaces, then bourgeois households, where it will be ridden by sullen children playing sulky quintets. But pianos and violins will never really be tamed, because there's always something about violins and pianos that frightens people, something that disturbs them, because violins and pianos are horses.

ARKADY WHO COULDN'T SEE AND ARTEM WHO COULDN'T HEAR

Some years ago, attempting to collect material for a still-unwritten book, I was travelling through Russia by train. The trains were long and overheated and smelled of pickles and unwashed clothes. It was difficult to find a seat where I could read or sleep undisturbed, but on leaving a city whose name I no longer remember I found a compartment with two men who were spending the long journey building a wooden house from matchsticks.

I didn't introduce myself, but watched as they carefully placed one match on top of another, using the tiniest bit of paste to hold their model together. The train ride was far from smooth, and I was amazed by the skill with which they kept their work standing. They spoke to each other in quiet, low voices, and I struggled to overhear what they were saying. Despite my reasonable knowledge of Russian, I could understand nothing of their conversation, and when I finally found they were not speaking Russian at all, but Komi. This language, they told me, still spoken by a few thousand people in central Russia, was the language they had been born into and the one used in the town to which they were now returning. They hadn't been back for many years, they said, and were trying to remember their birthplace by constructing a model of it.

As they spoke, each weighing the other's words as carefully and intently as they placed the matchsticks alongside each other, I couldn't help but notice the marked physical similarity between them. They were twins, they told me, the more talkative Arkady three minutes older than his quiet brother, Artem.

They were thin men, curiously built, with long square bodies and short legs, but both moved with a careful grace, their slow and deliberate gestures reminding me of mime artists or expert craftsmen. When I asked how long they had been building their model, they looked at each other and smiled. All our lives, said Arkady, all our lives.

The house we grew up in, he continued, was made of wood. So we build from wood, added his brother. They had a supply of matchsticks (still plentiful in an era in which smoking on trains was commonplace), but nevertheless worried they would one day run out before their work had been completed. Though the house was wood, it was a fine one, they insisted. Many of our neighbours looked down on us from the heights of their new tower blocks, but our parents would have nothing of this living in the sky. They were not modern people, our parents, said Artem.

Their skill with modelling was notable. Each match could be bent or split and placed in such a position so that, once named, it became exactly the thing it represented. They used their long fingers to indicate completed parts of their work to me, and as they spoke each simple coupling of sticks became the well, the vegetable plot in the garden, an abandoned cart or rusting car.

Arkady pointed at the model of a man holding a rifle. Our father, he said, was a hunter. It wasn't a pastime, said Artem, it was his job. He caught animals for us to eat, and when he was lucky he would trap and kill enough to sell to the butcher or at the market. When we were small, there was always plenty, said Arkady. Once, though only once, he caught a bear, said Artem. The meat was tough, remembered Arkady. It tasted like beef, said Artem. As the city grew around us, there was less for him to catch, they told me. Some rabbits, but they went quickly. Arkady said a word in Komi, but Artem corrected him before I had a chance to ask what he had said. It's not true, Artem insisted, there were never dogs. He never hunted dogs. We never never ate dog.

The twins had the smell of Russia on them, as did the whole train, that particular odour of timeworn sadness, vegetable decay, and vodka seeping from skin pores that used to be so typical of the country, and after a few days travel, I myself had begun to acquire the smell. I wonder now if it was this gradual change that allowed me to see what should have been obvious from the start: namely, that Arkady was blind, and Artem was deaf.

I had noticed that Arkady did not look directly at the person speaking to him and had taken his evasion of eye contact for intent listening, but I could now see the milky cataracts that clouded his dark eyes. Artem, meanwhile, watched whoever spoke to him intently, not out of politeness, but hanging his gaze on the speaker's lips in his efforts to read them.

Artem remembered the wolf. It slunk around the tower blocks, he said, near the garbage bins and the scrap of land where other boys played football. I was the only one who saw it, he said. It had come in from the forest after a hard winter, and kept coming for days. I fed it whenever I could steal some food from the kitchen.

It was a dog, said Arkady. He never saw a wolf, it was a stray dog.

I know what I saw, said Artem.

They took two matchsticks, slit them with the sharp blade of Arkady's penknife, then bent them like knuckles to fashion a small, four-legged animal, the burnt stub of the match its head. A dog, repeated Arkady. A wolf, muttered Artem, and each touched the figure, and it became as real as any wolf, or dog.

I have not mentioned the fourth inhabitant of our compartment. A red-faced Russian had joined us at some unmarked stop deep in the night, clutching a bottle that remained a third full no matter how much he drank from it. He slept soundly for the first several hours, but later woke and unwrapped a crumpled copy of *Pravda* to find a dried, salted fish, which he set at with repulsive sucking noises. His repast finished, he produced a pack of cards and began to play all by himself. The cards had unfamiliar markings, and I could not discern the rules of the game he played so intently and alone. Over the next few days he became more gregarious and started up conversations, of which I understood little, though Arkady and Artem nodded and laughed politely. He cajoled us into playing a game that he called *durak* and consisted of trying to rid oneself of all one's cards. I found the rules complex and confusing, though the others found it hilarious, especially when I became the *durak*, or fool. At a certain point the train slumped to a halt, and to my relief the game ended. The twins fell asleep, but the man remained half awake, losing himself once again in his solitary game, which he claimed he had to finish before he arrived.

The twins remembered the time their mother had gone sledging at night and added a sled to their model, on a hill formed from a balled-up sheet of newspaper. She had crept out one winter night with her sister, the twins in bed but awake, listening to their young mother, who had taken a tray from the kitchen to speed down the icy slope that rose behind their house. Her laughter that night, they remembered, was the most wonderful thing Arkady had ever heard, and the most beautiful thing Artem had ever been told about.

Somewhere in the middle of the vast emptiness the train ground to a halt and did not move again. I looked through the window to see nothing but endless birch forest, then looked again a few hours later, somehow hoping the view might have changed, but it hadn't. A harried conductor pushed his way through the train telling us we had been blocked by a heavy snowfall, and that it was possible we wouldn't move again for several days.

Blind Arkady snapped the blackened head from a match and placed it at the foot of the newspaper hill, and they remembered the time a meteorite had landed in their garden. It wasn't a meteorite, said Artem with the deliberate speech of the deaf. It was part of a spacecraft. When we were young, continued Arkady, we wanted to be cosmonauts. Every boy did at the time. There was a street in our town, he said, that ran between the new blocks called *ulitsa Kosmonauta*. One of the buildings had a huge mural on its side showing our brave pioneers of the future: the scientist, the soldier, and the spaceman. It was red and gold, said Artem, and shone in the sun. When I was a boy I thought it the most beautiful thing I had ever seen. We learned about Gagarin at school, said Arkady, but our mother told us he wasn't the first. There had been many more before Gagarin, concurred Artem. They died out there in space like the dogs, and nobody ever spoke of them. Sometimes parts of their craft would fall back to earth and land in the Siberian tundra or the endless forests of the Urals, and if anything was found what was left of them would be given a quiet burial in cities that were left unmarked on any map. This was what landed in our garden, said Artem, laying his finger on the tiny fragment of cosmic *disjecta membra*. Some, though, he continued, are still out there, endlessly circling the earth, their withered bodies still wearing their protective suits.

The train stayed where it was, in the lee of the gigantic snow dune, and time slowed. The twins continued with their model, while our companion drank, chewed at his piece of fish, and played cards. Sometimes we slept. When Artem was asleep, I asked Arkady how his brother had become deaf. Our father was not a violent man, he said, but he did have many troubles. Once he came home in a rage and beat Artem around the head. The bruises soon passed, but he was never able to hear again.

In one part of the garden they had laid a small pile of completely burnt matchsticks, curled and blackened threads that threatened to disintegrate into ash. This is to remember the time the house nearly burned down, they said. When I asked how this had happened, the twins moved uneasily. We try not to remember the time Arkady began to drink, said Artem, and the time Artem got God, said Arkady.

It was after he had gone blind, said Artem later while Arkady slept. He was angry, continued the younger brother, and turned to the one-eyed devil of the bottle. I asked Artem why his twin had such rage in him. 'Because he had been cursed with blindness,' said Artem. 'My brother turned away from God, as I turned to him.'

I asked Artem how he had gone deaf.

'I was born like this,' he replied, and rapidly continued his brother's story. The Komi religion, he began, is very different to Christianity. For us the human soul, which we call the *lov*, has a double, its *ort*. The *ort* is born with each human being and gives a premonition of death to the soul. After our father had gone away and our mother had died, each of us began to believe that we were the other's *ort*. With that, Artem took two matchsticks, broke one into uneven lengths, and added it transversally to the other to fashion a simple patriarchal cross. I went to see the priest, he said. Our parents had never taken us to the church, and once inside the waxy smoke of the candles mixed with that of the incense swinging in the censers, and the light that reflected from them onto the icons on the rood screen, gave me the feeling I no longer lacked a sense. The paintings of the saints and angels up above on the inside of the dome reminded me of the cosmonauts mural, he said, and through them God spoke to me.

At that point in his story, his brother woke and heard us speaking. He slowly passed his fingers over the model until they rested on the cross Artem had placed in a corner of the garden and made to remove it, but then faltered. No, he said, it plays its part in the story, after all.

I do not know if I began to drink when I first thought my brother was a sign of my own death, he told me later as deaf Artem slept, or if it was the drink that made me think so. For the Komi people, he continued, the land of the dead is located far to the north of this world, beyond all the mountains, rivers, and forests. After death, each Komi has to cross a river of tar. According to our sins in this world, we are given various means of doing this: for some there will be an iron bridge to walk across, for others perhaps only a wobbling broom handle, or, in the worst of instances, a mere cobweb. I drank until I could see the river, but never found how I would cross it.

As he told his story, the train began to move again, in short urgent shunts at first, then gently gathering speed with a slow sigh. Up and down the carriages, the other passengers let out a muted cheer, waking Artem.

When God found me, he said, I stopped believing in the tales we had been told. God made everything pure and clear for me.

And so the drink for me, added Arkady.

Our companion, the fourth man whom we had almost forgotten, lost as he was in drink, game, and sleep, cried out, *To the god of the bottle!* then laughed and took an enormous draught before going back to his cards.

I asked what happened after the soul had crossed the black river. Did it enter heaven?

No, Arkady continued, his blind eyes fixed on an uncertain point in the distance. Should the soul be successful in its crossing, it then has to climb a steep mountain made entirely of ice in order to reach heaven. This is only possible if the person has led a good life and has strong fingernails.

In the old times people kept their fingernails, Artem said,

like we keep matchsticks. They were buried with them, said Arkady, should they need them. I looked at the twins' fingernails, which were clipped short but looked as thick and strong as horses' hooves.

The fire began after Artem had spoken to the priest, Arkady told me later that night as his brother slept. Artem asked why despair existed in the world, and the priest told my brother that God had granted him just enough despair for him to marvel at the rest of creation. Without despair, the priest said, beauty would not exist. As Artem walked home he had an illumination: he realised that only God should exist in the world, and that he had to destroy everything that was not God.

Either Arkady or myself fell asleep at that point, I remember with difficulty, lost as we were in the night and travel and the telling of tales, and when I later awoke I found Artem looking at me, apparently taking it in turns with his brother to keep a vigil over their creation.

The fire began, quiet Artem told me, when Arkady fell asleep in a stupor and dropped the end of his lit cigarette into a vodka bottle. He was lucky only his eyebrows were singed.

They were both awake the next morning and smiled at me as I returned from splashing cold water on my face in the tiny washroom. Now we drink only tea, they said, and we do not pray. Despite their claims, I found something unconvincing in their breezy assertion and suspected that deaf Artem still felt the pull of the gleaming domes and thick incense, and that blind Arkady still dreamed of the pop of the bottle top, the peppery warmth as the spirit went down.

Days passed in travel, the train being frequently held up or slowed by the weather conditions. The drunk finished his oblique game of patience and grew increasingly agitated, attempting to engage us in conversations, which were incomprehensible, or card games, the rules of which were no less so. Some buildings on the twins' model grew bigger, yet others seemed no nearer completion than when I had begun my journey over a week ago. As I sat awake one night, reading a collection of Russian tales less fantastic than the one that was unfolding before me, I finally realised why. The brothers were indeed taking turns to keep a night watch over their work, but that was not all. As Artem slept and Arkady stayed awake, I saw him not adding to the model, but taking away from it. With a careful deliberateness he removed all but a few of the matchsticks his brother had put in place earlier that day, scraped the glue from them, and put them back in their bag. I said nothing, and pretended to read. Later, Arkady slept and Artem stayed awake, and again, through the corner of my eye, I watched him adding a few pieces, yet at the same time subtracting the few his brother had added. In this way, I realised, their model would be ever-changing and never-growing. It was never meant to be completed.

The next morning the snow clouds had lifted, the air was brighter, and for the first time in days the train sped through the birch forests in the manner it had been designed to. I watched the trees pass as quickly as the hours, keen to get on with my journey, to arrive somewhere.

But then, just as I was thinking of what I would do when I arrived (a hot shower in a friendly hotel, the first proper meal in ages at a good but simple restaurant, a deep sleep on a firm mattress), a squeal of brakes ripped through the silence and the train slammed to a halt. Bags were thrown from the luggage racks onto our heads, we were launched into unlikely and improbable clinches, thumps and cries were heard from up and down the carriage, the card-player's bottle slid and smashed on the floor. Yet as all this happened we each kept our eyes on one thing only: the model slid a few inches across the table until it teetered on the precipice, but it did not fall. When the train juddered back from its sudden stop we all looked upon this small miracle.

'Not even an earthquake could destroy our home,' said Arkady, and everyone laughed. Then the drunk picked up the stub of his bottle, raised it above his head, and smashed it down into the centre of the model.

The train driver, it turned out, had braked so as not to hit a deer crossing the track. The deer had fled unharmed, but the train was compromised in such a way as to necessitate a termination at a dull industrial city, still many miles from our intended destination. We crawled on for a few hours before reaching an old station where a steam locomotive sat at the end of a siding, unmoved for many years, and were told to disembark.

The twins picked up their small cases, the polythene bag filled with matchsticks, and the wreck of their memories and stood on the platform in the bright morning light, tiny flakes of slowly falling snow shining around them. They would wait for the next train, they told me, and I watched them recede as I walked off to find a hotel.

'Goodbye,' they called. 'Remember us, and never trust a woman called Olga.' They waved to me and I waved back, each of us in perfect time.

Recently, I was back in the city where I had last seen the brothers and spent the few hours between trains walking its icy pavements and admiring the steep banks of snow that rose up from the sheer white river. I thought of Arkady and Artem and worried about disposable plastic lighters imported from China. Should the twins, wherever they were now, still be constructing their model, they would surely run out of their raw material.

On the way out of the city, I noticed some wooden houses, not dissimilar to the one they had begun and never finished building. Its windows were broken, some parts of it were boarded up with plywood and cardboard rather than elm or birch timber. A faded bouquet of flowers hung in the window casement and the house leaned madly, sinking into the snow like a ship running aground a thousand miles from the nearest sea.

THE *NEVA STAR*

There is a ship moored in the port of Naples that has been there for three years. In all this time, it has moved no more than a few inches, backward and forward, from side to side. This is not an entirely unusual situation, as there are many ships in many ports around the world that have found themselves abandoned by bankrupted owners, impounded by national authorities, deserted by soon-to-be ex-magnates, orphaned by unpaid bills. In Genoa there is a ship that has been there for five years, and in Venice one for seven. An old ship moored in the port of Naples for three years is not an entirely unusual situation. All over the seafaring world there are ships that are flying the flag of the Bolivian and Mongolian merchant navies.

The *Neva Star* is a large dry cargo and tanker ship, designed for sea and river use with a reinforced hull so it can break ice from Arkhangelsk to Murmansk. It is registered in Odesa and is as rusty as a nail. It is 115 metres long and has three thin decks. It is painted orange and white. The bottom part of the ship is orange, the upper part white. White and rust, orange and rust. The ship was built in Romania thirty-five years ago and has since travelled over twenty thousand miles, sailing from Valletta to Leith to Rotterdam to Port Klang to Laem Chabang, then back to Odesa where it began and, now, to Naples.

Of the crew of seventy, sixty-seven have disappeared. There are now only three sailors on board. The three sailors have been there for three years. Three years plus the three months they spent arriving in Naples from Odesa. Nobody knows what happened to the captain.

Sergei, the first mate, passes much of his time thinking of his wife Masha. He has lived with Masha since Saint Petersburg was called Leningrad. Once, many years ago, Masha had the chance to leave Russia and go to Israel. She packed her small black leather bag with everything she had and got on the tram and sat there circling the canals of the Fontanka for hours. Late that evening, she arrived back home. Sergei opened the door of their flat to find her standing on the doorstep crying. He had absolutely no idea why she had arrived home late, crying. This is one of the things he remembers as he passes the many days lying on the small bunk in the same cabin he has slept in for more than three years. He still doesn't know why Masha arrived home late that evening, her cheeks wet with secrets.

Sergei, another of the sailors, occasionally finds himself thinking about the time when, returning from a voyage to Cuba, he and his old friend the first mate Sergei took the trip from Odesa up to Saint Petersburg to visit Sergei's hometown. He stayed for a week with Sergei and Sergei's wife Masha in their small flat on the twelfth floor of an apartment block on Ploshad' Musžestva. Their flat was as small as a ship's cabin, he remembers, although the view from the window was always the same. Now, out of the small porthole in his cabin on the *Neva Star*, the view is always the same.

Sergei hasn't seen his wife for five years. They met at a party when they were eighteen and married soon after. Three months later, Tatiana disappeared. Sergei wasn't worried. He heard she had gone to Moscow and moved in with a wealthy importer-exporter, and decided it was best to leave it there. Still, he sometimes misses her, even though he now thinks he never really loved her. He thinks about Sergei's wife Masha, and the time when he stayed in their tiny apartment and the time when he kissed her once, very quietly and very quickly, while she was cooking potato soup in the kitchen. He wonders what the Italian girls are like. Before he disappeared, one of the other sailors—a Romanian called Sorin—told Sergei about a friend of his who'd been stuck in Porto Marghera. He'd jumped ship and married the first girl he'd met, a Venetian. Sergei remembers reading somewhere that Venetian women are supposed to have webbed feet.

The third sailor is called Sergei. Sergei has often been tempted to chuck it all in and go onshore. If he got caught onshore, he'd risk getting sent back to Ukraine immediately and not being eligible for any pay for all the time he had spent on board the *Neva Star*, should it ever get out of Naples. This is why all three sailors stay on board. If they left, they would be summarily repatriated and forfeit any right to monies accruing. Sergei has heard that there are other Ukrainians in the city, though, and is sure that if he could find them he could set himself up here in Italy. Even though the others don't know it, Sergei has found eight hundred American dollars in a small bundle that smells of dried sweat in a worn brown envelope under the bunk in the captain's cabin.

There are three sailors left on board. They are all called Sergei. There is enough canned food on board to last them, they have calculated, for up to five years. They've been there for three years. They have enough canned food to last them another two.

Sergei, solid, dependable, practical, and realistic, thinks it's better than the time he got stuck in Antwerp for three months. Even though he's been here for three years now and has never set foot on the land that is but a few metres away, he already knows that he likes Naples more than he liked Antwerp.

Here, the sky seems closer, heavier, bluer and thicker, especially when he thinks of the pale Baltic sky, distant, thin, and airy. He sometimes wonders why a boat registered in Odesa should be called the *Neva Star* and, despite his solid, realistic practicality, can think of no other reason than some vague intention to make him feel even more homesick.

They've been there for three Augusts, when the bright heat is enough to split paving stones. It creeps on board like an animal and rubs around them, sticking to them like fur coats they can't take off. They've been there for three New Years, watching the fireworks over the city and listening to the other ships sound their horns at midnight, then celebrating their own muted vigil a week later, still obeying the Russian calendar, with one of the few bottles of sovetskoye shampanskoye that they have carefully stored away for New Year, Easter, and three birthdays every year. They have already drunk all the vodka that was on board.

Sergei dreams all the time, and not only when sleeping. He dreams of the sun sliding down the steps in Odesa, of his family and the house where he grew up. He dreams of being trapped on board the *Neva Star* for three years, of being on board this very ship, a dream that is inseparable from reality, and this dream worries him. It worries him mostly because in this dream there are only two of them, not three. He wonders what has happened to Sergei in his dream, but there's no answer. He has a bad dream where Tatiana's new husband comes looking for him armed with divorce papers, which turn into a gun which turns into a dead fish. He dreams of Masha's trapped eyes and women with webbed feet. Waking, he remembers his dreams, then remembers the story: the travellers on the road to Emmaus. Wasn't it supposed to be two travellers who imagine a third? *Who is the third who walks always beside you?* Wasn't that the line? He wonders why he's dreaming the opposite.

When they go out on deck and look at the city beyond the docks, they see rows of white cement buildings and a wide road where cars speed past at all hours of the day and night. At night the road is dimly illuminated with fuzzy light, and they can see a few people loitering in the blocked yellow spaces under the shadows of the tall buildings.

Sometimes they are incessantly together, eating, sleeping, breathing, and shitting in rhythm, all but holding hands for weeks at a time in a near hysterical attempt to escape the vacuum of solitude. They have played more games of chess with each other than they can remember. Sergei always wins.

At other times they have spent months hardly talking to each other, going about their business (such business as they have) alone, spending time lying eyes open on their bunks, not consciously avoiding each other but speaking little so as not to exhaust topics of conversation, reading slowly so as not to finish the few books they have, moving slowly as if trying to conserve time, breathing slowly for fear they'll use up all the air they have left.

Sergei has taken to disappearing when he thinks the others won't notice him gone. At night, usually, though sometimes during the day when it's quiet, he stretches a plank across the water and walks onto land. The solidity of the stone quay under his feet throws him off balance and makes him feel sick. He steals into the city, crossing the road with its deadly roaring traffic and scuttling up through the alleys that permeate the tall, ugly buildings. He is soon lost and has to ask a group of Polish people under the main station the way back to the port. He sees plaster peeling off the old buildings in the centre like the skin off his own sunburnt lips.

Fearing the thieves he has heard about in Naples, he keeps tight hold of the bundle in his pocket, fingers clenched around the notes. He had worried about looking out of place or conspicuous and wonders why nobody takes any notice of him. He wonders if he has taken on a different appearance, as if his time on the ship has made him look like one of the natives. Not even the Poles were surprised to see him. He regrets not asking them if they had any Ukrainian friends, and promises himself he will come out again and find them, and ask them.

He doesn't want to wait too long. He is starting to feel anxious. When he was counting the captain's dollars he heard the click of the lock opening and a throat clearing in embarrassment before seeing Sergei slip away from the door. Since then, he has moved the worn brown envelope to a new place every day. He spends a lot of time thinking about where he's going to put it next.

Once a journalist came to visit them and asked them lots of questions about life on board the ship. The journalist brought greasy cardboard boxes with pizza in them, and bottles of beer. A few days later there was an article in the local paper, complete with a photograph showing them sitting in the deserted canteen embracing each other and grinning, but they never saw it because the journalist didn't send them a copy of the paper, even though he'd promised to.

This also meant the feverish negotiations that were going on to sell the ship and release the men also described in the article took place completely unknown to them. In oak-lined rooms with green leather chairs and air-conditioned offices with marble floors in London, Lisbon, Athens, Istanbul, Liberia, and New York, emails had pinged back and forth, containing details of agents and auctions, terms and conditions, get-out clauses and loopholes, prices in euros, dollars, and sterling.

Sergei has often thought about trying fishing. He looks down at the narrow canal of dark water that surrounds the ship and wonders what may be swimming around in there. The froths of white and brown foam and the sickly rainbows of shiny oil that occasionally slide across the green-black surface aren't encouraging, but he's seen people fish in water much worse in Petersburg.

He rigs up a rod made from a broom handle and some twine weighed down with the broken bottom of a vodka bottle, which he also hopes will act as a fly, and perches on the edge of the *Neva Star* and sits there for hours, fishing without catching anything. Once, he sees an enormous grey cod, evidently lost, but it doesn't bite. Every now and then he pulls up the twine to check. There's nothing to use as bait. He thinks that may be why he doesn't catch anything.

He wonders what any fish who might live in the waters of the port of Naples would eat and what he would find in the belly of a fish he caught when he gutted it with his penknife. Bones, little fish, jewels.

As he sits there fishing he thinks about the money he saw Sergei counting and wonders where it came from and where he's hidden it now. He sees a girl sitting on the deck of a yacht passing in the distance, and she reminds him of the mermaid he saw sitting on a rock in Copenhagen. She reminds him of Masha, and he wonders what his wife is doing now. He wonders why she left him after his friend Sergei had been to visit, and why he never told Sergei she'd left.

After the article in the newspaper, the sailors became a minor tourist attraction. Small groups of people came to look at them and wave to them from the shore. They would wave back, and the two groups would shout things to each other in mutually incomprehensible languages. After a while, though, the novelty faded, and people stopped dropping by. Now they've become such a fixture that people don't even see them there anymore. In the future, people will tell stories of the three Russian sailors who spent three years on a boat in the port of Naples.

Sergei thinks that if anybody should ask him where he lived now, he would still say in that house in Odesa. That's where I live, he'd say, there in that house with its high windows and wooden floor and the old stove we light in the winter to keep warm. That's where I live, with my mother and my little sister. He would get out the picture he keeps with him and show the house with its moulded ceilings and crumbling arches and the dark entrance hall where the old dežurnaja who never speaks lives. Nobody asks him where he lives.

Sergei knows that this is siren land, that he is stranded in a city founded when the mermaid Parthenope fell in love with one of Odysseus's men who ignored her by blocking his ears and sailing right past her. She was so heartbroken she cried until she died and her body was washed up on a rock here.

Rust wears the bow, salt eats up the paint on the hull. There are no seagulls to make any sound, as there is nothing to scavenge. The only sounds you can hear on the *Neva Star* are the distant roar of traffic from the city, the creak of fatiguing metal, the sea sweating oil in summer, the gnaw of advancing decay.

Sergei slinks out after dark and heads back to the station where he met the Poles. At night, there is no one there but a few drunks. He tries asking them if they know any Ukrainians round here, but nobody answers him apart from a man with a face so red and swollen Sergei fears he is about to explode. He recognises Sergei's accent, tells him he is from Moldova, and they start speaking in Russian. Sergei says he's been stuck on a boat in the port for three years. The man with the red face tells him a story that he's heard in Naples. Once there was a boy called Cola Pesce. Cola Pesce loved diving down and swimming for hours and hours in the waters of the bay of

Naples. His mother got fed up with him doing nothing but sploshing around in the water all day and said that if he didn't give up he'd turn into a fish. That's why they called him Cola Pesce. Cola dived deep down into the water and let a huge fish swallow him up. Then he travelled all over the world, under the sea, in the belly of the fish before eventually getting out his knife and cutting himself free. When the king heard about Cola Pesce's talent he demanded to see him. 'Tell me,' he asked the boy, 'What does the bottom of the sea look like?' and Cola Pesce replied that it was filled with gardens of coral, wrecks of ships, pieces of amber, phosphorescent fish, and precious stones scattered about among the bones of drowned sailors. The king told him to go down again and bring up some of the treasure for him, but Cola immediately had a bad feeling. 'If I go down again,' he told the king, 'I'll never come back up,' but the king insisted, and Cola went down again. In some versions of the story he takes down a handful of lentils with him, in others a piece of wood, in others a drop of blood, and he says that if this thing rises to the surface before I do, then I shall be dead. The lentils, the piece of wood, the drop of blood float to the surface. They're still waiting for him to come back up.

Sergei gives the red-faced man some of his money, and heads quickly back for the ship, making sure he doesn't get lost on the way.

Shipwrecked on board a ship, stranded afloat under a flag of inconvenience, they listen out for visitors bringing them good news. They hear only unquiet ghosts, snoring sailors. The emails, once chattering about the sailors' fate, have stopped their pinging now. Any contracts are nothing more than ink fading on sheets of curling white paper piled up on dusty office floors or chewed up by the long sharp teeth of shredding machines. Agents, intermediaries, and insurers have long since gone bankrupt, or moved on to the cases of other ships, stranded in other ports.

Every day Sergei walks out onto the deck of the *Neva Star* and looks out across the bay. He fills himself up with the luminous intensity of the big silver mornings, watching the rigs and funnels of other ships, the hunched cranes and walls of containers on the docks, the wide flat mirror of water in the port basin and the broken-topped triangle of Mount Vesuvius in the distance. He thinks it's one of the most beautiful things he's ever seen, and thinks about how it would be to live here forever and spend every morning looking out at that looming shadow. He thinks about the money that has been stashed away and gets moved every day and where it came from and what will happen to it. He wonders how many Poles and Ukrainians and Romanians and Russians and Turks and Cubans and Albanians and Portuguese and Indians and Bangladeshis and Filipinos there are in the city, how they got there and what they do there. He wonders how many other sailors are stuck on those other ships in other ports and how they got there and what they do there. He ponders over what may or may not have happened to the captain. He remembers his brief wife Tatiana, Masha's face after he'd kissed her, and Sorin's friend's Venetian wife. He thinks about legends of mermaids and mermen, at home neither in the sea nor on the land. He thinks that being on board a ship is like leaving and leaving and leaving and never arriving anywhere.

SISTER

In April 1992, shortly before I started taking photographs, my sister went missing. I have never seen her since.

We were twins, me and Marie, though identical only in our solitude. She was as blonde as I am dark, her skin as dark as mine is pale. As if we'd been half swapped, bits of us crossed over in the womb. Chalk and cheese, they'd say, refusing to believe we were even related, not trusting our common surname, our strange, silent language. We never invented any code or secret babble to protect our world but always knew what the other had done, was doing, or would do. Even though I haven't seen her for so long now and don't know anything of her whereabouts, I still feel her close sometimes, a part of myself missing, a phantom extra limb.

I couldn't say when I started to realise she was different. All of us are mysteries in our way, and her way was close enough to mine as to make it hard for me to see. We walked the same pathway, though looked in different directions. People asked if I worried about her or if she was okay and I'd just nod and say *Sure, it's nothing*, not seeing what others could. There was nothing strange about her to me, but I often make the mistake of thinking I'm normal.

Her disappearances were little ones at first, tiny moments when she was, then wasn't, there. All children do it some way or another, those instants when they make themselves invisible, testing a distracted parent's anxiety a little longer every time. But Marie was different, she had a way of slipping into and out of being, reappearing at your shoulder the moment you started to notice. At the foot of a shady garden, in a supermarket, on a beach in the summer: the places where children often go for minutes at a time, and Marie would do no different, but then she'd begin to do it at home as well, absent herself just long enough so it was realised and then, the moment people began to worry, reappear.

Until one day she didn't. But that would happen much later.

We never spoke about growing up. I just thought it would happen, but my sister didn't. She existed in her own space and her own time, letting the world move around her while she stayed fixed, exactly where she was, choosing whether or not to be there.

Age didn't touch her. She never did the things I did, go through phases, get spots or boyfriends. When we were teenagers she started not turning up to things or arriving hours too early. She never really found the knack of telling the time, never wore a watch. It got her detentions, but she didn't mind, indifferent to whatever time she had to stay. Recently, looking through some old pictures, I tried to find us, but there is no image in which her face isn't blurred, slightly out of focus or only half in the frame. She was too slow or too fast for the shutter, resistant to chemicals.

It was later, after I'd gone to university and she'd stayed with our parents, drifting and circling, that I started to get phone calls at strange times of night, the ring in the hallway at 3:00 a.m. ignored by flatmates knowing it would be my crazy sister. Her voice would be slow, as slurred (I thought) by sleep as I was, emerging from the murky night and the dirty receiver, or delayed as if she was calling from the other side of the world. Other times I'd hear a hyperactive babble, impossible to follow, the words piling up on themselves. I thought it was drugs, but it wasn't.

She came to visit once, turning up unannounced early one morning, the sun hardly risen. I had no idea how she'd arrived or where she'd come from, but by then such behaviour was typical. She walked into my room as though she knew the place already and built a nest from a pile of books in the middle of the floor. I can't remember how long she stayed, a week, maybe more, but I do remember she never went out, nor spoke to anyone else. I don't even remember her eating. She passed the days opening all of my books, sometimes poring over a page or a word for hours, other times flicking through as if she could read them in seconds.

'How do you know,' she asked, 'when these things are happening?'

'I don't know what you mean.'

'The things in these books, they're stories . . .'

'Some of them are—'

'. . . which happen in the past . . .'

'Well ...'

'But when you read them, they're happening now.'

'That's the effect they can cause—'

'So how do we know when anything's really happening?' I was baffled at the time, put it down to her oddness, tried to explain something I'd read about a *remote* tense, the one we use to talk about something that happened time ago, or that is hypothetical, or even when we just want to be polite, but she'd gone before I could finish.

I didn't see her for years after that. Mother told me that she'd disappear, sometimes for days, sometimes for weeks, then reappear again with no word, as if nothing had happened. Marie was always vague about where she'd been, but seeing as she was healthy and clean and not apparently troubled, my parents never worried.

Until the day they found her staring at the clock on the kitchen wall, in tears. 'It's just ... *not right*' all she could say, panic rising in her voice. She couldn't tell the time at all anymore; I wasn't sure she'd ever been able to. They took her for a brain scan, fearing some kind of stroke, but it showed nothing. Doctors sighed, gave her antidepressants and telephone counselling. Meanwhile, Marie gave up on the idea of time altogether. She seemed much happier, Mother told me.

It was '92, late March, the year finally starting to turn, when I got another call. 'She's not well.' She never is, I thought, but listened patiently to my mother's descriptions of Marie's ever-more frequent absences alternating with long periods locked in her room, then accepted her request to go to the old house they kept in the country, the one that had been my grandfather's and where we'd spent summers as children.

I hadn't been back there for years, always too cold even in summer, shot through with the smell of damp and rot, miles from anywhere, useless for a hurriedly arranged rendezvous or weekend escape.

Marie was already there when I arrived, sitting on the massive broken-springed sofa we'd jumped on as kids. There was a large stain on one end of it, the result of a bottle of red wine and a row between my parents. She didn't look up when I walked in. I went to put the kettle on but there was no electricity.

'There's gas,' she said. 'I've fixed the gas. I usually put a pan on the hob.' The water took an age to boil, and we sat there in silence. My mother had told me the doctors had looked at her again but found nothing wrong with her, so they couldn't put her away. 'But best for her not to be on her own,' they'd advised her. I handed my sister some tea and searched through her things: the shambling clothes she'd had for years, a worn-out toothbrush, a packet of fluoxetine, unopened. Also, a stack of books, dog-eared and stained, lay on the floor of the tiny upstairs room she always chose. I recognised some of them—ones I remembered reading as a kid. She must have brought them from my parents' house, where they had been shelved on the landing or stacked in cardboard boxes in the attic.

She seemed no different, so I settled myself in for a long stretch. Little of the looking-after my mother had requested needed doing. I didn't resent the intrusion, was doing little myself at the time and had enough money to last me a couple of months. Marie could take care of herself, I had no worry about that, food always a minor but annoying essential for her, a piece of toast or some old fruit enough to keep her skinny body from vanishing completely, though I'd often find her having breakfast at midnight, then asleep at noon.

When asked, which I did with decreasing frequency, she'd tell me she was fine, but as the days wore on I realised she wasn't. That's why I stopped asking, the words made no sense to her. It was a twin thing, I suppose, knowing the desperate sadness in her, touching it myself, but having no idea where to go with it. Other times she would move so slowly, be sitting so still, she would take hours to drink a cup of the tea, which had become the only thing she'd eat or drink, the liquid so cold when it got to its dregs. Hours became seconds, and seconds could shift into hours.

I went out most days with the excuse of needing to get milk or cigarettes or a newspaper, but mostly just for my sanity, rambling the long way round to avoid the narrow roadside, cutting through long-forgotten footpaths and the edges of muddy fields. After a week, maybe ten days, I returned to the smell of burning. The kitchen was filled with smoke and an acrid stink, but no flames. Marie had put her pan on the hob and forgotten about it. This was what I'd worried about having to do with my mother one day, not my sister.

She was on the sofa, cross-legged, a book open on the space in her lap.

'I only just put it on,' she said when I confronted her with the burnt pan, 'a second ago, just as you were going out.' I'd been gone two hours, at least.

Many of the books she'd brought with her had now shifted down the stairs and into the main room. I was sure there were more there than a week ago, as if they were breeding. A couple sat, smoke smelling now, on the kitchen table. Reading was the only thing she could manage to do. Sometimes she would stare at one page or even a single word for hours, others times flick through the pages as though she could read an entire book in seconds, like I remembered her doing all that time ago.

'All these books,' she said, 'their pages are empty, perfect blanks until you begin to read.' Madness is as madness does, I thought: Who could say she wasn't right? 'When we were children,' she went on, 'I read a book full of smoke and fire, shadow and flame. I only remember a boy coming through a doorway, fearing what he'd find in the room. That's all. I tried to find it again later, looking at pages and pictures and jackets, picking books up and flicking through them, trying to find an illustration or a turn of phrase I recognised, something that brought the story back to me, but even though I came close, often, I never found that book again, never could recall what happened in it, what the story was, or, worse than the story, recapture the atmosphere it filled me with. I read every book there, but it wasn't. It wasn't there anymore. And always, since then, I've been going back and looking.'

I got on with scrubbing the pan, it was the only one we had, and resolved not to let her alone so much. It was in the days that followed that she began to disappear. Only slightly at first, those tiny things she had always done, slipping out of view even though she was in the same room, reappearing just as you'd notice her missing, nothing but a voice at my shoulder at first, then materialising, and vanishing again as I acknowledged her presence.

Every madness is logical to its owner. Marie had gotten lost, gone mad, call it what you will, when time had ceased to mean anything to her. Even if she never moved, she would never know where she was.

Sometimes, if I remained completely still, holding my breath and slowing even my pulse as far as I could, I could see her perfectly. She'd slide into view and then out of phase again as I drew breath, let my heart beat and blood flow. She moved not at twenty-four frames per second, but just one.

It wasn't all slow stillness. There were times when the film sped. I kept a close watch but she vanished anyway, and these were the times I wondered, I worried, if she had moved into another slipstream, time now passing for her so quickly she vanished from view.

How else could it have happened?

The time I was out in the garden, minutes, at most, then came in to find the house had moved on years. The mould had grown, the season outside the window had changed, and all the clocks had been smashed.

There had only been a few in the house, all wound down or batteries exhausted. One on the kitchen wall, one in the hallway, another on the mantel in the living room. Their insides mixed on the floor as I walked in: the different ages of chronometry scrambled. The shards of a small black plastic battery pack, springs and cogs, shattered glass, twisted hands and, so sad, the broken faces.

'Watch,' she said. 'They were all watching me.' I couldn't tell if her tears were of happiness or relief or distress. 'On your wrist.' She pointed. 'It's watching you.'

Time was her enemy, stretching out forever or forcing its entire weight into tiny moments of her life. For Marie every second was an eternity, every eternity a second. She was there from the big bang until the eventual heat death of the universe, sitting on the sofa in that room, looking for a story whose ending she would never know.

The next morning she'd gone. Or perhaps it had been the one before that, or the day after. I can't remember anymore. There was no car abandoned near a bridge, no pile of clothes neatly folded on a beach or a riverbank. There was no bag ever found in a left luggage locker at an international station.

TROUVÉ

To pass the time while we waited I was telling Anna a story I'd heard about a guy in Turkey who gets wasted one night then wakes up in a forest or something, unsure where he is. He gets up, dusts himself off, then stumbles across a search party, all in hi-vis, I suppose, with maps and whistles and stuff, and they're out looking for someone, so being essentially a good citizen, he decides to join them, to help out. Only then—

'He hears them calling his name? He realises it's him they're looking for?'

'Ha, yes. That's it.'

'I've heard that one before,' she said. 'Only, when I heard it, it was in Iceland. A tourist had got off the bus and changed her hat, or something.'

'I don't get it,' I said. 'She's changed her hat and they think she's lost?'

'Something like that, yeah.'

'And she joins the search party for herself?'

'Yeah.'

She didn't seem interested in what I thought was interesting so I shut up and went to have another look at the arrivals board, which said my friends were going to be twenty minutes late so I sat down again.

'What's that film?' I asked, 'The one where the guy slowly realises it was him, that he was the one who did it?'

'I don't know that one,' she said, and then we were quiet again for a bit.

And then she said, out of the blue, 'Same thing happened to me once.'

'What?' I said. 'You got lost and found yourself?'

'Kind of, yeah.'

I thought she'd go on to tell the story, but she didn't. Anna was odd like that.

There was a pause for like five minutes or something.

'What's that film,' I asked, 'where they're sitting around waiting for someone to arrive?'

'Waiting for Godot.'

'No. A film.'

'I don't know,' she said, 'but there was this time, a few years back now. Maybe twenty. God, ages ago. I was in Paris, was passing through, en route from somewhere to somewhere else, can't remember where. I used to travel a lot, work, that's what it was usually, but sometimes I just went roaming. Out with the camera. See what turned up. That kind of thing.' Anna was a photographer and I'd known her since school, though she wasn't a photographer then. 'I remember having one eye on my watch and worrying about getting to the station or the airport on time.'

'Like now?' I said. We'd run because we thought we were going to be late to meet my friends but then we got here on time, and now they were late.

'I always worry when I've got a flight or a train to catch, so I decided to walk. Walking's the best way to kill time. And it was Paris—a great city, the *best*, for wandering and watching, so they say, though when I get there I always find it too crowded and everything's, I don't know, already seen. Like I'm looking at pictures of the place and not the place itself, even though I am actually, literally there.'

'I haven't been there for ages.'

'I went looking in shops just to get off the pavements. I liked the window displays, they always put such care into them, even if it's only a chemist or a fruit and veg place, though when you go in there's nothing but an unfriendly assistant. Clothes shops. Bag shops. Even if I'd wanted to buy something I wouldn't have been able to afford it. Hat shops. Shoe shops. But then I wandered off the Grands Boulevards, found myself in one of the puces in Clignancourt or Saint-Ouen or somewhere near the Sorbonne, perhaps, I'm not quite sure how I'd managed to stray so far. A shabbier neighbourhood anyhow, not that there's anywhere in the centre of Paris that's exactly *shabby*, but you know, less glitzy, and there was this row of little shops selling prints, old books, pictures, frames, mostly junk, though everything had a hefty price tag.'

I wondered if we should have another coffee even though it was late and wished they served booze here, but she didn't seem bothered.

'I once went to a Pret in Switzerland where you could get a beer,' I told her.

'Will you remember them?' she asked. 'Will they remember you? How long has it been since you last saw them?'

'Ages. I haven't seen them for ages.'

'You might not recognise them.'

'They might not recognise me.' I sent a text saying *How will I recognise you?* with a laughing emoji, but they didn't reply.

'So there I was,' she said, 'Looking through piles of old postcards, I love doing that, especially when they have writing on the back, even if I can hardly ever read it, just a name sometimes, or a little message. Who were all those people, that's what I ask. Who were they? There were a couple of cardboard boxes under the table, stacked up on top of each other, both packed with photographs, mostly newer ones but a whole mix, some really old, dating back to the twenties, thirties, maybe, stiff cardboard frames, faded as soon as they'd been taken, then some from the fifties or sixties, smaller crimp-edged pictures of families out for the weekend, picnics, weddings. Weddings featured heavily. Back then they took pictures of things they thought should be memorable, the passages of life, that kind of thing.'

'The things we think are going to be important.'

'Yeah. But a lot of people sitting in cars, too. Not driving, just sitting behind the steering wheel grinning.'

'There's a picture of me and my brother like that, somewhere.'

'Then there were all these seventies polaroids with boxy white edges and woozy colours, jug-eared children in bad knitwear. And then some from the nineties, unloved.'

'How do you know they were unloved?'

'You can tell. More time has to pass before they get interesting.'

Time wasn't passing. We still had ages to wait, so I sent them another text and they still didn't reply.

'I wondered how the pictures had got there,' she said.

'House clearances.'

'Broken relationships, no longer loved pictures of no longer loved lovers.'

'Now they'd just get deleted.'

'No more old photos.'

'They'll all be on hard drives somewhere.'

'Bricked phones.'

'You can never really delete anything.'

'And then, and this is the thing, there was this clutch of photos of some grim-looking family event, and in among them, I was there. Me. There was a picture of me there.'

The lights went up to show the café was closing. I never know why they do that. You'd think it'd make more sense to turn the lights off. Everything went strangely bright.

'You?'

'Yeah. Me. Strange, but I didn't find it that surprising at the time. Looking back on it, it's obviously *fucking* bizarre. But. At first, just for a second, I wasn't sure, couldn't be. Someone who looked a lot like me, that's all. So I looked more carefully, and it was quite definitely, absolutely definitively, me. I remembered the black jumper I had on, under that leather jacket I still have somewhere. I'm looking at the camera, so I must have known that someone was taking a picture of me. It wasn't a stolen shot, a street photography thing, something someone had snapped of me sitting in a café or in a bar somewhere. Because that's where I seem to be. You can tell by the lighting, and the people around me in the background, though their faces are out of focus so you can't see who any of them are. I look like I was probably on my own. Or maybe with the person who took the picture. Who was someone who knew what they were doing—the focus and framing were perfect. I looked pretty good in it. Imagine a picture of me out there, I thought, unknown to me, and I was looking terrible. A stupid thing to think at such an odd moment, but.

'I asked the man in the shop how much he wanted for the picture. Dix pour un euro, he said. I told him I didn't want dix, I only wanted one. Un euro, he replied.

'Regard, I said and pointed at the picture, C'est moi. I smiled, he smiled, but didn't say more. I gave him the euro. I put the picture between the pages of my notebook so it wouldn't get creased, then I put the notebook in my bag, and I left.'

'What happened then?'

'I kind of forgot about it.'

We decided to go out for a vape, or maybe we were still smoking then, because they clearly didn't want us in the café anymore.

'What's that film?' I asked. 'The one where the guy starts getting pictures of himself through the post? I mean, someone is sending pictures to him, like, surveillance pictures. What is that film?'

'I don't know that one,' she said. Then we were quiet for a bit.

'Now that I think about it,' she went on, 'I'm not so sure that was what happened. If I think about it again, harder, I might have gone to Paris for a show, I'm sure it was Paris, that I am sure of, there was an exhibition there that I'd wanted to see but it was vaguely disappointing, very small, and all stuff that I'd already seen in books. Sometimes I just forget things completely. I think I might have been there with someone else as well, someone who knew the place and had led me to that row of shops in that particular area, knowing that would be where I could find what I was looking for. But for the life of me I can't remember who it was. I'm not sure if it was that row of shops either. Maybe it was somewhere else entirely. What I do remember, though, now that I tell this story again, is that after leaving the shop I decided to do the obvious thing, the thing anybody else would have done, and I turned back, went into the shop again, and asked the man where the hell he'd got these pictures, this picture in particular. I held it up as I spoke.

'He didn't know. Je pas, he said. I don't work here often, he said, just every now and then. I'm looking after the place for my uncle. I don't know where he got them from.

'Is your uncle around? I asked. Can I talk to him? En vacances, he said. Away for a month.

'I went back to the box and carefully looked through the rest of the pictures to see if there were any more of me. This makes no sense, I thought. No sense at all. I hoped there'd be some from the same moment, to cast light on it, put it into context, to help me remember, perhaps, but more than that I found myself hoping there'd be other pictures of me too, other versions of myself, as a teenager, as a child, as a baby, as a grown-up. Maybe there'd be ones of me in the future. I thought there might be all of me in there, that all of my life might have ended up in a cardboard box under a rickety table in an upmarket junk shop.

'There was nothing. I told myself I'd go back when I had more time, but I never did. I sat on the train, or the plane, maybe, and I looked at the picture again, really hard this time. How young I looked. How much time had passed. And here's the thing—I felt I'd been reunited with my former self, that person I used to be, whoever she was, and it felt good, but at the same time, even though we'd been reunited, I had no idea who she was, who I was, where I'd been, what I'd done, while this young woman had sat there in a cardboard box, or had been off and had loads of adventures and done god knows what for all those years. When I got back home I slid the picture between two books on my shelves. Now I can't remember which books. And I have quite a lot of them.'

'Is that it?' I asked. 'Is that the story?'

'That's it,' she said. 'That's how I remember it. That's what happened.'

I went to have a look at the arrivals board, and it told me their train was due. We walked over to the end of the platform and watched it roll in. Late-night trains are often half empty, but this one was busy, and as the doors opened and people spilled out I scanned the faces coming toward me, trying to spot the friends I hadn't seen for so long.

ONE ART

An absence on his desk; a slight disturbance of the expected. He'd mislaid his keys, that was all. Such things happen. They weren't where they should have been, not where they usually were— the worktop, the kitchen table, the drawers in the hallway. Not in his coat pocket, nor the one in his jacket. Not by his bed, nor on the side in the bathroom. Not stuffed into his jeans, not lying on the floor. An annoyance, no more. He went out anyway, leaving the door of his house unlocked.

• • •

At first it was nothing. A sound in the bottom drawer of the chest next to her bed. A tiny rustle, a creak. It's the old wood expanding or contracting, she told herself, rolled over, and went back to sleep.

• • •

His phone went after that. This was more significant: keys could be cloned from the landlord's masters but a phone contained messages, contacts, months' worth of notes. He ran a trace of the places he had been since last seeing it: the supermarket, the pub, the corner shop. Nothing remarkable. He wondered if it were hidden in the flat, along with the keys, but a thorough search turned up nothing. It had been stolen, he grew certain, though when he came to report it to the police, he had no idea who might have taken it, or when. The report would be carefully filed and soon forgotten, he suspected. He should back things up, the police told him, copy them, clone them, double them, store them on a stick and in the cloud.

As he walked home he found himself preferring the idea that the phone had simply slipped from his pocket somewhere, dived down a drain or into the river. Made a bid for freedom. Gone.

• • •

It was later that day when she'd gone back up into the bedroom that she heard it again, a little louder this time, barely audible, but definitely something there. She hoped to god there weren't mice in the house, decided the best thing to do for now would be to ignore it, shut the door, and hurried back downstairs.

• • •

Nothing else then, not for some time. Some petty irritations, nothing more: never being able to find a cigarette lighter, no loose change for cash-only bars, never a pen that worked, or a pen at all. It was only later, looking back, that he saw a pattern.

• • •

The next night, as she settled in to sleep, it was there again. She heard a sigh, surely nothing more than an echo, the room breathing her voice back to her.

• • •

Clothes were next, hats then gloves then scarves and jackets, rapidly followed by socks, shoes, shirts, undies. Once he'd started to see what was going on, the process sped up. His flat grew emptier. Knives and forks from the cutlery drawer, plates, cups, saucers. Showering was difficult as the soap and shampoo disappeared, but then one morning he found the shower itself had gone, so that problem was solved.

Without even a towel to wrap around his waist, he walked back into the living room, unwashed, to find the sofa gone, the table and chairs too.

He turned around to find the rest of the room empty.

• • •

It was in the early hours, shapes just forming in the light, that she heard it again.

Help me, it said. I'm in here. Help me.

• • •

Apart from the books, that was. The books had stayed. He left them there, not daring to touch or hardly even look at them.

• • •

She slept at a friend's house the next night. The walls are as thin as paper in that house, she told her friend. You can hear every neighbour's row. Sounds sometimes come up from the street, her friend told her. Sometimes people walk past and I can hear what they're saying perfectly, as if they're in the room. That night she slept well. Everything was silent.

• • •

He slept on a bare mattress in an empty room.

• • •

As she walked home the next day, she tried to remember the voice she'd heard but it was always different in her memory, sometimes whiny and wheedling, other times deep, dark, and assured, more of a threat than a request for help. Sometimes it was a child's voice, other times an old woman's. The fact it was always different, she told herself, meant it was clear that she'd imagined it.

• • •

He began to wonder if he himself would disappear too, and constantly looked at his hands, his skin, his face in the nighttime window to check he was still there. And he was, his skin sagging, the whiskers on his chin and the nails on the ends of his fingers still growing and filling with grit.

• • •

When she got in, the silence in the house was as thick as the dust. She walked slowly, trod carefully for fear of waking it. If I'm quiet, she thought, then it will be quiet too.

• • •

Toward the end, he opened a book, one both of them had loved, and as he leafed through its pages he saw the words disappearing as he read. The picture he had kept, the one of them together, was now only a white piece of paper in a silver frame.

• • •

Help me, it said as soon as she walked into the bedroom, the voice as clear as her own. *I'm in here. Help me.*

'What do you want?' she asked.

'Help me,' it said. 'I'm in here. Help me.' She could open the drawer, or she could leave it there. She could choose to help, if she wanted. 'Help me,' it said again. There was no pleading in its tone.

• • •

He soon found himself living in a neighbourhood in which no one walked the streets. The houses opposite began to lose their features. White curtains shrouded their windows, all the stones turned grey. The sky vanished. It became a blank white sheet, unchanging from day to day. He tried to write down what was happening, but on waking the next morning found the pages of his notebook empty again.

• • •

She got a man from the charity shop to come and take the drawers away the next morning. That night it was silent, and a part of her missed the voice. She sleeps soundly now, and has no fear of empty rooms, knowing that one day she will hear that voice again. Help me, it will say. I'm in here. Help me.

A BRIEF HISTORY
OF THE SHORT STORY

1. THE FRENCH SHORT STORY

On a day that the newspaper he was about to buy predicted as being cold and overcast but would instead turn out warm and bright, M. Roger Grenier, a semiretired office overseer at the Department of Public Finance, set out on his morning walk. He had taken to the habit some six months earlier following his departure from full-time work in an attempt to give his day shape and purpose: a stop at the baker's, where he would still be called *maître* and waved to the head of the queue; another at the newspaper seller to get his *Figaro*; then a possible stop for coffee; and finally home again to read and reply to the day's correspondence. Should time permit he would begin work on his *grand projet*—the writing of his memoirs, with which he planned to fill the empty days as he sailed into old age, decrepitude, obsolescence.

Meudon, at that time, was a Parisian suburb where solid farm buildings of Normandy stone appended by rough wooden lean-tos were being surrounded by paved roads, electric lighting, and the well-appointed, wooden-shuttered, three-storey houses of the bourgeoisie who were moving out of the city centre. Paris was pestilent, filthy, filled with thieves and beggars; Meudon offered clean air and the smell of healthy farmyard but an hour from the Grands Boulevards. Grenier had chosen the upper storey of a small house with a modest garden from where, should he lean out of his study window and crane his neck to the left, he could see the gold dome of the Invalides where he had worked for the previous thirty-five years, and to where he would not return.

M. Grenier did not have to do this. He did not have to buy his own bread. He could have sent out for the newspaper, or had it delivered. He had no need to walk out this unexpectedly bright morning along Rue des Galons to make some humble purchases. He knew he had the wherewithal to employ a second domestic, but other than having his housekeeper (Madame Avenel, the rawboned and sullen but efficient widow of a local fishmonger) visit once a day (except Wednesday and twice on a Sunday), he had decided to occupy himself personally with day-to-day tasks. He was, after all, aware of the limited nature of his savings and wanted to spread them as far as possible into his future, which (some nights, lying awake) he would admit to himself was unmeasurable. He was, after all, aware that his empty days had need of shape. He was aware (some nights, lying awake) that he had need of human contact, however brief, in his loneliness.

So this morning Grenier stopped at the newsstand and bought himself not only his customary *Figaro* but also today's *Petit Journal*. Though normally unmoved by the *P'tit*'s diet of gossip, scandal, and entertainment, the so-called faits divers, the unforecasted sun on his shoulders sparked a desire to engage Mme Avenel or the baker or the café regulars in gentle conversation, and a copy of the *P'tit* would surely give them something to talk about, and he wished to savour the pleasing brevity of the moment.

Newspapers acquired, he turned back and stopped at the café on the corner of Avenue le Corbeiller and, after a superficial scan of the finance pages of the *Figaro*, casually unfolded the *Petit Journal* and turned to the faits divers. He worked his face into a not-unself-conscious smile, attempting to portray a serious man indulging in harmless whimsy. After all, his memoir (which he had thought of calling 'An Unremarkable Man' before being sage enough to realise this would not attract many readers) probably needed some leaven. Maybe he could take some ideas from the *P'tit*.

A story caught his eye. Less than a few hundred words, its details scandalous enough for the average *Journal* reader, thought Grenier, though little of substance. He hadn't seen it mentioned at all in his (albeit brief) read through *Le Figaro*, so there couldn't be much to it. A certain M. Valse (though he was also known as 'Bayard' or 'Erikson') had reportedly returned to Paris after fleeing the United States, where he had gone some twenty years earlier in an attempt to find his fortune (though the article also hinted that he had perhaps left France not only in search of the Golden West but also to avoid some unnamed unpleasantness he had been involved in). Valse (or whatever his name was) had prospered in America until his business associate (a certain Mr. Delaney) had gone missing in unexplained circumstances. Valse fell under the suspicion of the doughty Arizona lawmen and—perhaps more significantly—Delaney's formidable wife, who had also put out a considerable bounty for Valse's eventual deliverance unto the law. Grenier shifted uncomfortably as he read. There were more details, ever murkier. Some hint of bigamy, a dubious will, a contested inheritance. His patience was soon done.

There wasn't really a story there at all. Merely a jumble of unsupported facts and a lot of speculation. Grenier regretted his purchase. Had he wanted an hour's distraction he should have found something containing a conte or a nouvelle, something by Hugo, Balzac, Gauthier, Zola, Sand, Daudet, Flaubert, Mérimée, or (best of all) Maupassant. Any one of those writers would have given shape to such a story. He wished for a skilled pen, the careful placing of each element, the timing of the slow reveal to a crushing truth. Something shining yet bitter, something that would stick the knife into the guts of this city.

The sudden flash of bitterness passed, he folded the *Journal* and turned back to the *Figaro*. If only life had a shape. If only life had the sense of a story.

'Ahoy there!' A second annoyance in this otherwise placid day. M. Grenier's former colleague Vallin entered the bar. They called him *le marin*, as he claimed to own a boat and frequently spoke in a ridiculous nautical slang he appeared to have picked up from reading third-rate swashbucklers. The only thing that had disappointed Grenier in his move out to Meudon was the discovery of this man living not a few doors away from him. Vallin le Marin pulled up a chair without invitation.

'After the reward?' He jerked his thumb toward the *Petit Journal* lying on the table, folded open at the story Grenier was trying to forget.

'Ha! Never thought about it. Some trash I picked up to pass the day.'

'Thought it wasn't your kind of thing, old dog,' continued Vallin. 'A far more serious character you were. No one ever really knew what to make of you.' Hardly pausing for breath, he carried on before Grenier had a chance to ask quite what he meant by the remark. 'Still, be useful, though, eh? Nice wad of cash the lady's putting up.'

'I'm not sure what you mean, Monsieur,' lied Grenier.

'This reward!' continued Vallin, picking up the paper. 'Two thousand dollars—how much is that?'

'About ten thousand francs,' said Grenier too quickly.

'Ten thou! Shipshape, I'd say!' Unwillingly, Grenier found himself thinking how far ten thousand francs would go. Almost his annual salary, when he'd had one. 'Half the city's looking for him. Let's see what we can do. Here we go. Height, weight, distinguishing marks: about a metre eighty—hmm, very average—slim, with a moustache. He's going to have given that the chop, though, isn't he? Not daft, this one, I'd say.' Vallin looked at Grenier a second. 'You've still got the moustache, haven't you? Not thought of a change?'

'And why would I do that?'

'Y'know, with what happened . . . it's good to have a change sometimes. Put up a fresh sail.' Grenier shook his head. 'No, perhaps not. Anyhow, this chap—black hair, no distinguishing marks. Sheesh. Not giving much away, are they? Needles and haystacks. Drops in oceans. Could be anyone. Come to think of it, could be you! That'd be something, wouldn't it?'

'I don't know what you're suggesting, Vallin.'

'No, of course. But a joke, in poor taste. Pardon me. Did they ever . . . I mean, has anything more . . .?'

This was what Grenier had wanted to avoid, inevitable as it was. A cloud had hung around him since Mme Grenier's disappearance. The police had found nothing, nor the private investigators his father-in-law had employed, yet the scent of scandal was enough for it to be gently suggested that he should tender a resignation, on grounds of health, which would be accepted with a small pension in return.

'No. Nothing more.' Grenier stood to leave, taking the *Figaro* with him and pointedly leaving the *Petit Journal* on the table. At least his story had never made it in there, as far as he knew.

Outside, a cloud passed, and the temperature had fallen. The day was turning out as predicted. Across the street a photographer was setting up a camera. He seemed to be focussing on the old farm-house, which stood, semi-abandoned, just behind the café—the point, no doubt, to make some kind of comment on the passing of the old. Yes, the old was passing, thought Grenier, and so much the better to let it pass. He marvelled how this day that had started so brightly had been tainted by a petty scandal rag, and also at the pre-cision with which a squalid story had so subtly traced and marked his own life.

Perhaps he should have shaved his moustache off, taken his money, and gone to America himself. But no, there was nothing so remarkable about him.

Grenier pulled his hat down hard and turned to leave at a crack. He did not want to be photographed. He realised people might mis-take him for the wanted man, or that he would later appear on the photograph, a shifty blurred figure escaping from the scene. Maybe they would trace him and come for him, hungering for money more than justice. He shuddered. He wouldn't want to be questioned by the police again.

It had been worth the indignation of their enquiries, the shame of them dredging the river and the raked walks up and down the railway lines. It had been worth his father-in-law's silent scorn, the sudden cessation of chatter when he walked into his office. All that had been better than telling them she'd run off with a junior officer young enough to be the son they'd never had.

Maybe Emilie was there too somewhere, in the background

of a photograph, another bystander to history. If she were, he hoped he'd never see it.

Grenier rued the lack of a clear ending to his story. Could one of his favourite writers do it justice? Clear endings were so little like life, after all. This afternoon he would finally sit and start the memoir, if only to make himself the main character of his own life, and not a minor character in someone else's.

2. THE RUSSIAN SHORT STORY

There was nothing remarkable about him.

Vassily Cherdak had suspected it for years and now, on the eve of his forty-fifth birthday, was certain. The contents of his kitchen cupboards underlined the fact: a half-empty jar of bitter coffee that was drying up, various collections of tea bags, only the black and linden varieties drinkable; just enough sugar to sweeten approximately one cup each for the guests he was expecting later that afternoon; one good bottle of vodka (to be saved for the guests), and the dregs of a cheap one.

But why should there be anything remarkable? What was good about being 'remarkable,' anyhow? All 'remarkable' meant was that when you walked along the street people would point at you and *remark*. On what? His big ears? His long nose? His utter lack of any other defining characteristics? It mattered little, it seemed, as long as they *remarked*.

He walked the circuit of his apartment, five paces in each direction, entirely normal for a man of his standing. Identical to the apartments above, below, and on either side of his. And the ones in the next block, and the one after that. The sofa, chairs, carpet, and thinning Afghan rug. All normal. He looked at his bookshelves and thought of rearranging them so the most impressive volumes were more prominently displayed. They were something that could be remarked on—not him, his books.

He'd shaved off his moustache for the occasion. That would certainly attract a remark or two. Or perhaps his party guests wouldn't even notice. It wasn't even a party, really, just drinks. He hadn't reminded his colleagues it was his birthday, hoping they'd remember.

Average height, weight, looks. No dramatic scar lining his face, nor tattoos indicating covert membership of a secret society. The fact he didn't look remarkable bothered him little. It was the fact that, over the course of forty-five years, he had *done* so little that was remarkable. Remarkable meant they ought to remark on him with praise and admiration. 'See him over there? Yes, Vassily Cherdak, that's him. You know what he did . . .?'

He wasn't sure any of the four would arrive anyway. On a Saturday afternoon they'd all have plenty of other things to do. Would one bottle be enough? He couldn't offer the cheap stuff, and anyhow that bottle seemed to be empty now. He decided he'd have to get another, and some cakes. It was his birthday, after all.

The lift cut out at the third floor, not bad, some days it didn't work at all. He walked the last few flights down and grasped the chill of the day as he went out. Past the unremarkable three blocks—snow still on the waste ground between them, this late in the year just chunks of ice now—as far as the corner where two drunks sat on the step of the produkti, not moving as he opened the double doors to go in and be welcomed by the smell of sour meat and cheese. Vassily hoped the redhead would be at the counter, the one who always had a little smile for him. He'd tell her it was his birthday and she'd let him have a bottle of the good stuff, the one that was officially in defitsit but could always be made to appear with the right words and a few extra notes. He'd have to promise her something if he didn't have enough extra cash, though he didn't know quite what as his job allowed him to grant few favours to members of the general public. Offering to get her poem or story published in an august journal would work, but Vassily doubted she were of that inclination.

He could always promise something both of them knew he couldn't deliver. It didn't matter—these days everyone knew a promise was an exchangeable currency, something only ever to be traded and never cashed in. It was their version of capitalism. It would get them all in the end, capitalism, he thought. Assuming the vodka didn't first.

It could be a story from Gogol: an imaginary promise that gets passed around as though a coin. Kafka, even, though he wasn't sure if Kafka was allowed at the moment—it all depended on quite where they were with the Czechs. An anekdot, one of those stories based on a tale or some barroom gossip. You were usually safe with those as long as they only poked fun at officially sanctioned targets, but even those were always moving.

He was in luck; the redhead worked her magic without need of unsustainable promises, though it did leave Vassily lacking even enough small change to get the humblest of pastries. It didn't matter—as long as they had drink and conversation it'd be enough. Though they might be scarce on the conversation front too. The only people he'd invited worked in the same office as he did, and conversation between them was little and stilted at the best of times. What would they talk about out of the office? He had thought of inviting some others before realising he didn't know anyone else.

He thought he'd better buy a newspaper, get himself up to scratch about what was going on, be able to offer some informed opinions as to the controversies of the day. He could talk about books for hours but didn't know if his guests would want to discuss anything that sailed into potentially dangerous waters, not least the embarrassment when someone pretended to have read something they hadn't.

The newspaper kiosk stood in the small square where there was little space for anything other than the massive statue of Pushkin. They were all supposed to like Pushkin; Vassily was secretly never quite sure why. *The Bronze Horseman* had bored him senseless at school, and when he'd got to university he'd joined a racy clique whose shared abhorrence of the man who was supposed to be 'our everything' had brought them together. Gogol would be more apt,

Kharms dangerously so. Chekhov would be best: gentle, accommo-
dating. He thought he could really get behind a country where there
was a statue of Chekhov in every town square.

Defitsit of paper, so no *Isvestia* today, and he was buggered if
he was going to spend his last bit of cash on the deadly dull *Pravda*.
There was a copy posted on the boards around the tram stop so he
headed up there, a nip to keep him warm on his way. Break that seal,
why not? It was his birthday, after all.

When he got there he found Khlestakov had given a speech
that had made it onto the front page, and needed another nip.

Vassily genuinely remembered the 1960s as having been
warmer. The thaw hadn't only been metaphorical, he was sure. His
memories were of endless Leningrad nights, sovetskoye shampanskoye, vodka that didn't taste of gut-rot, and being able to say almost
anything they wanted. Khlestakov had been the lead mouth in his
university circle, a group of would-be writers and intellectuals who
talked much, drank more, and did little. Little that was remarkable,
anyhow. They were going to refound literature from the base, accept
foreign influence yet temper it with the finest of Soviet steel. They
talked about wild cacophonies of discordant voices, *dzhaz* and their
great forebears in the Russian avant garde traditions. The word was
to be put to the service of revolutionary peace. They called themselves 'The Black Square,' and aimed to do for literature what that
picture had done for painting. Vassily liked the painting, it had sim-
plicity and honesty, and never felt it was much like what the others

were trying to do at all but kept his opinions to himself, a habit he had learned young, found useful, and stuck with.

He had hung out with them a lot, but had been careful never to get too close. Khlestakov had only been able to get away with it because of his high-ranking father. Vassily himself would never have been so bold. There had only been one serious talent out of the lot of them: Lidiya. Lidiya Zinovyeva had once taken him into her confidence and shown him her tales about growing up on a farm in the Baltic. One had made him laugh, another cry, another—the best— both at the same time. It was her, he realised, who made him think of those times so warmly. He was never sure if he were in love with her, or with what she had written. The last time he'd seen her she was getting onto a boat on the Neva, midnight and still light, a bottle in either hand.

He never heard from or of her again. He supposed she'd got married, gone off somewhere, become a schoolteacher or something like that. As far as they were concerned, he'd disappeared too. He still heard of some of the others, minor novelists or critics with lesser or greater success. Khlestakov most of all, making the best of his connections to end up becoming secretary of the Writers' Union and free to pronounce on whatever came into his head, as long as it was all cleared with the old men first. The speech flagged on today's *Pravda* was on 'The Duty of the Soviet Writer in Changing Times.' He would have been put up to it by Andropov himself, thought Vassily— Khlestakov had pronounced on the same subject before, the said duty often changing in accord with the times, changing or not. It wasn't engineers of human souls they were looking for now; it was middle managers.

Damn, this day had been going so well, with getting the good bottle and all. And now this.

His own disappearance had been unremarkable. After university he'd got a job as a journalist on the arts beat for the local rag in the provincial city where he'd stayed ever since. Still warm from the thaw he'd filed a 'lost generation' piece on Bulgakov, Akhmatova, Mandelstam, and Platonov, not realising they were headed right back into the deep freeze of history, which would have been exactly where he ended up too had not his editor been wise enough to spike it immediately and merely get him demoted to proofreader at the local branch of the Ministry for Mining. In a country like this, it was difficult to predict the past.

He'd had enough, he went home—the lift was working as far as the seventh floor, at least—boiled water for tea, then worried he wouldn't have enough for later so helped himself to another small tot, sat on the sofa, and found a book to read. A French story. You knew where you were with the French. Not like the old Black Square group. He wanted harmony and clarity of structure, some faintly lurid tale of bourgeois corruption, a nexus of money, fakery, and social status anxiety, possibly with romantic betrayal thrown into the pot. All perfectly permissible, nothing that would get him in trouble with anyone, as evidenced by the recently translated state-sanctioned anthology he'd bought the week before as an early birthday present and would now sit down to enjoy, with a glass.

Several fact-checking and punctuation-adjusting years later, he'd been discreetly approached about another job in the ministry. It seemed his diligent work had not gone unnoticed, and now they were looking for someone who could carry out much the same work, but with an eye to content as much as form. It was only after some sideways questioning (an art that had grown to be second nature) that he realised they were looking for a censor. He was surprised by how potentially subversive reports on coal and mineral mining in the Voronezh oblast could be, at least according to the careful guidelines he was given. (The guidelines were regularly updated, often with minuscule ideological implications or linguistic turns, always needed very delicate interpretation, and were often given to being changed without notice.) Occasionally, and strictly unofficially, he'd be asked to comment on literary matters, potential publications by one of the state-approved houses (probably because, he suspected, the boy who held the official post was functionally illiterate). He always hoped that one day a collection of stories by Lidiya Zinovyeva would cross his path, but it never did. What would she be doing out here, anyway?

The French story started quite well. It was by a writer he didn't know, the tale of an unremarkable man who read a story about a crime in a newspaper and somehow found himself obscurely implicated in it. He soon got lost, though, and put it down to tiredness and the lousy translation (why was one character speaking like a sailor?) instead of the small glass he'd taken. It wasn't his kind of story after all, he decided. He didn't want patterns and symbols, parallels and connections. All this talk of impostors, doubles, shady truth, and dubious morality. Dostoevsky would have done so much more with the same material. Fyodor would have sought the real truth in the story, lambent and eternal. A story should show the distinguishing features of the race, what was remarkable about the Russians.

He'd been working too hard, maybe. He had become his own censor. He deserved a snooze. Half sleeping, he imagined himself a character in a work of great Russian literature, but then realised that when history came to be written, it would be about the writer whose work he was censoring, and not the humble censor. Who would speak for him?

He roused himself and tried to get back to the story. Doubles and cheats, petty criminals and officious bureaucrats, it wasn't the stuff of Dostoevsky but more of the old stories his grandfather had told, country tales and mess hall ribaldry. They had a life in them, those things, a vigour. Back to the anekdot again. He thought about looking for some Zoschenko or Dovlatov but was too tired to get off the sofa. Besides, he didn't know if they were safe at the moment, and it wouldn't do to have them lying around when his guests finally showed.

He should write his own story, see if he could get it past himself: an anekdot based on a joke he'd heard about a man trading a false promise in order to get a bottle of vodka. Yes, that was the Soviet Union: it wasn't the lack of freedom, it wasn't the lack of food—it was the drudgery. This, he thought, this was what Gogol would be writing today. The Russian soul: a soul capable of drinking a litre of vodka and withstanding huge quantities of utter, inescapable, relentless boredom. This was the true meaning of the Black Square: sheer bloody unending indisputable boredom, overwhelming everything and everyone. It pressed down on him as he fell asleep.

He dreamed of Lidiya's hands as she boarded that boat on the river, beckoning, one bottle for him. He dreamed he was reading a story, so much more than a mere anekdot, about an invitation not taken, a life not lived, with an ending he could feel coming, unpredictable and inevitable.

A ring on the doorbell woke him. His guests were finally arriving. He'd finished all the vodka.

3. THE AMERICAN SHORT STORY

When the 8.40 American Airlines from Tucson left dead on time, taking Sharon with it, leaving only her usual half-finished coffee behind, Jeff knew he'd never see her again. It hadn't been his drinking, as she'd said, he assured himself as he hit the ignition of the rusting hulk of a Pontiac (he remembered how she said she'd loved the classic aura of the GTO), hauled it out of the vast parking lot, and swung north onto the Nogales Highway, headed home, a home that would be empty now.

No. That wouldn't do. Five *w*'s and one *h*: that was the way to do it—who, what, where, why, when and a how. That's what he'd learned. One sentence, too. Had to be. Work it all into one sentence.

When the 8.40—

Does it matter what time? Could he just write 'plane'? Wouldn't that be too flat?

When the plane left Tucson—

That wasn't bad, actually, but still felt like something he'd have written in grade school. Surely it was the detail that gave it texture, realness, *life*. Those parentheses weren't working either. Getting it all into one ball-grabbing opening sentence, dropping the reader right in there wasn't easy.

He looked at the tangle of words again and realised it took even him several minutes to decode. Think: first principles—what's actually going on here? He didn't really know himself: Jessica had left him.

Sharon had left.

Would that work? No—who the hell was Sharon? Why? Where? Think about those *w*'s. 'Sharon had left.' That sounded like one of those European stories. And not in a good way.

First principles again. Where's the start? Where does this

story start? He couldn't remember where it started. When he'd met her, he guessed. That would be a pretty lame place to start a story, though, two lovers meeting for the first time. He couldn't even remember when he first had met Jess. She'd just kind of drifted into focus somehow.

She'd just kind of drifted into focus somehow.

Not a great start.

His sophomore year at Arizona State. She'd been in the World Lit class, he thought, or maybe just hung out with the other guys who were. When was the first time he'd really noticed her? The car, that was it.

She said she loved the classic aura of the Pontiac GTO.

It was a shitty piece of crap he'd been left by his uncle, but he had no other way of getting around so took it on only to find it cost him half the month's paycheck to keep on the road. Every month.

She hadn't even said 'classic aura'—that had been his idea, giving a philosophical-sounding concept to the simple fact that the rustbucket did at least help him pick up girls. 'Classic aura' was his thing—it was why he'd smoked Marlboro Reds and drank Pabst, even though they both grated his throat like an electric sander.

She said she'd loved the Pontiac.

Maybe that should be the first line. No specificity, though. Too vague.

Sharon had said she'd loved Jeff's old Pontiac.

That sounded like 'Pontiac' was the name of a dog. Or dirty innuendo.

Sharon had said she'd loved the classic aura of Jeff's old Pontiac.

Everything had to be in that first sentence. 'The first sentence should be a promise the story will keep,' his MFA tutor had told him. He liked that. That was a good sentence.

Maybe that could be his title, 'The First Sentence'? That was getting too clever. All that Barth, Barthes, Barthelme shit he'd had to read. He never could tell them apart. Though there would be those who would appreciate it being so meta. Some competition judges and small magazine editors liked all that PoMo shit.

He put down his notebook and hauled the Pontiac out of the vast parking lot onto the Nogales Highway heading north, heading home.

. . .

He was a strong lonely man pitted against the forces of the west.

A line from one of the first stories he had ever written came into his head, probably because a hefty wind started blowing grit and heat right through the old car. Right now he could certainly feel the forces of the west. Lonely too. Strong, maybe not so much. Even though he winced at the line now, he had to admit he still kind of liked it. It called up the things he admired, some of the best American stories. God, though, he'd never get into *Canyon Voices* if he wrote that now.

He got home, threw his keys on the couch, threw himself right after them, and fired up his computer. His *Mac*, he'd write: specificity. His *scratched MacBook Air*—best make it seem old, like he didn't have much money. He didn't have much money, though, especially now he'd be covering rent on his own.

He opened up his Facebook, Twitter, Insta, tried to see what was going on in the world. Not much. He realised he'd have to change his relationship status. Too soon. He scanned through various messages, none of which meant anything to him, clicked on news headlines, all redundant. He connected nothing with nothing.

She left.

She'd left.

The latter, maybe—that would pitch the reader into his post-Jessica world. He wouldn't have to write about her at all, just leave that as a given. A strong lonely man pitted against . . . what? Himself?

Maybe that was the way to go. None of this long sentence stuff, go back to Hemingway, Carver, Ford, lean, taut prose, as muscular and sinewy as he wasn't. He scanned the shelves for *What We Talk About When We Talk About Love* but couldn't see it. Jess must have taken it. Bitch. It'd been his copy, too.

He googled it. E-book cost more than the real fucking thing! Bastards. Luckily there was a ripped PDF of it. First story, 'Why Don't You Dance?'

In the kitchen, he poured another drink and looked at the bedroom suite in his front yard. The mattress was stripped and the candy-striped sheets lay beside two pillows on the chiffonier. Except for that, things looked much the way they had in the bedroom—nightstand and reading lamp on his side of the bed, nightstand and reading lamp on her side.

His side, her side.

He considered this as he sipped the whiskey.

This was too much. He thought about their—his—own bedroom. This was PoMo meta shit gone mad, and it wasn't funny.

It wasn't supposed to be, of course. This was what a great story was. *W*'s and *h*'s be damned. Patterns, reflections, traces. Coincidences that become real. Fiction hitting truth like a car crash. He checked the clock. He'd have to be getting to work in a couple of hours. He could stare at the internet, or the wall. He could have a drink. He could keep on writing the story. He could go out and get coffee.

He opted for the latter and decided to risk the Four Corners. Get out of the house, quit moping, engage. *Things happen to people who write stories, people to whom things happen write stories.* He'd read that somewhere, had scribbled it down in his notebook. He'd take the notebook with him, and a book to read in case it wasn't happening. It'd stop him checking his phone. Plus, reading a book was a good middle finger to people he didn't want to talk to.

A thick volume sat on the shelf next to where the Carver should have been, black spined, serious. *Twentieth Century Russian Short Stories.* It had been from the World Lit class, he thought, but he'd never read it. Maybe it was Jess's and she hadn't bothered with it. It'd do: the Russians—big themes, tightly expressed. That was what he needed. None of this small shit about yard sales and drink problems.

• • •

'On your lonesome today?'

'Yep.'

'What are you reading?'

'Um. Russian short stories.'

'Wow. Sounds heavy.'

'Just a latte, please.'

'Sure.'

He'd always had an eye for the cute redhead server, but today really wasn't the day.

He couldn't get on with the story. *'There was nothing remarkable about him'*—then why the fuck should I want to read about him? Who was this guy, anyway? No five 'w's and an 'h' here—the Russians clearly had different rules.

Not only didn't he get who the guy was, he couldn't understand why he'd invited these guys to his house party if he thought they wouldn't come. What was this? *Mrs* fuckin' *Dalloway* with vodka? One-man *Waiting for Godot*? It all seemed too distant to him, too vague. This was nothing like Carver.

Maybe it was just the lousy translation. Those sentences were way too long. So many words and yet he still couldn't get what was going on. He didn't trust translations. *Of course, you should really read it in the original.* Something that douche in the World Lit class had said when he was trying to get on with Chekhov. He was probably right, but really, am I going to learn Russian? Maybe it was the Soviet era this story was set in, it was just too distant to him. More specificity, more feel of the real. He wondered, seriously, how those guys would get on today—they might be regarded as masters, but in today's publishing climate no one would give them a hope in hell.

Maybe it was just his own lousy mood.

It wasn't the same: the Russians really did have stuff to deal with, huge struggles of oppression and conscience. Not only did your partner leave you, but you could also get jailed for writing a fucking story.

Oh shit. Ben and Nicole had just walked in. Not this, not now. Please don't let them see me. He pulled the book up to his face.

'Josh!' 'Sup, dude?'

'Hey! Nuttin' much.' He and Ben still had this thing where they tried to talk like old-school hipsters, even though they were both nearly thirty now.

'Where's Jess?' Nicole was looking around.

'Um. She's away for a bit.'

'Okaayy,' said Nicole with a rising inflection that showed she thought something clearly wasn't okay. 'Everything cool with you guys?'

'Um, yeah. Sure. She had to go see her mom about something.'

Nicole's concern relaxed.

'Okay, great. Maybe I'll message her later. What you reading?'

'Um, a Russian short story.'

'Okay. Any good?'

'Not really.'

'Wanna come sit with us?'

Josh squirmed.

'I think he's trying to write something, honey—let's leave Salinger here to it!'

'Thanks, Ben.'

'No worries.'

Josh stared at the page but couldn't get back to the story. It seemed to have just stopped. He hated stories like that. He wanted stories that *ended*, not just stopped. Maybe he hadn't read it right; his attention was shot. He could see them from the corner of his eye, huddled, lowered voices, Nicole's anxious glances cast in his direction, Ben shrugging it off as if it were nothing. He wondered if Jess had talked to Nicole. Probably everyone knew already.

He dropped the book and went back to his own story. He put a massive black line through the entire first paragraph. He felt better. The story needed to be more real. It needed to have more weight. And the massive accumulation of detail wouldn't help that.

Maybe he should write about people other than himself. What if this were *her* tale? How would she tell it? Maybe he should make Sharon—Jess—the protagonist? Who owned this story? Maybe he was wrong to make himself the main character.

Maybe someone should have cancer.

Josh saw Ben get up and worried, but no, he was only moseying to the counter to pick up a copy of the *Tucson Weekly*. Nicole was looking at her phone. She was probably texting Jess right now. He watched them sitting in silence, like couples do.

Ben started guffawing, folded the paper, and showed something to Nicole. Nicole looked at it, then at Josh, then back again to the picture. Ben got up and walked over to him, waving the paper, still guffawing.

'Hey, Josh! Check this!' He slapped the paper down on the table.

'What is it?'

'Check this dude—he looks like you!'

Josh looked at the picture—a full face of a guy who, he had to admit, looked just like him.

'That's weird. He could be my dad! What is it?'

'This guy's offed his business partner—prob'ly—and gone missing, but there's no body so the cops can't charge him. The partner's old lady—the scary-looking woman, here—puts out a bounty for him. Old school. They reckon he's headed back to France, though. You're safe!' Josh looked at the picture again and felt a weird shiver. It did look like him, in about twenty years' time, maybe. Then again, he felt he'd aged twenty years in the last few days. 'Good job you shaved off that 'stache, otherwise they'd be after you.'

'Maybe I should turn myself in, collect the cash. It'd come in handy.' Nicole came and sat down opposite him.

'Leave it, Ben.' She took Josh's hand in hers and squeezed. 'Listen, are you okay, honey?' He stared down into his empty coffee cup, hoping she wouldn't see the tears welling. 'Things a bit tough at the moment, huh?'

'Um. Kinda. Yeah.'

'Wanna talk?'

'Nope.'

'Well, you look after yourself. Give us a call, any time.'

'Take it easy, bro!' Nicole led the way out, Ben shuffling after.

When he came to write it, later, soon, this afternoon or this evening or maybe tomorrow, he'd cut this bit out of the story.

Look at me now, he thought, I'm looking at a coffee cup, nothing more. That's the only thing you can put in a story, not a whole life, just a moment. Just a fucking empty coffee cup.

He paused and looked at the empty fucking coffee cup, and thought about his third-grade teacher, Brazil, digging snow from the porch when they'd lived back east, an Italian girl he'd once slept with and whose name he couldn't remember, his mother, dying of cancer. Jess. The kid they'd never had.

Scout, she was going to be. Or Atticus if a boy. He hated that book, but it was Jess's favourite. It didn't matter either way, though: it had never happened. Too soon. He wished he could have seen it, though. Him or her.

Maybe I could work that into a story, he thought.

Yes. Maybe that would be something worth writing about.

PROUD WOMAN,
PEARL NECKLACE, TWENTY YEARS

Proud woman. Pearl necklace. Twenty years.

He wrote the words on the board and sat with the chairs in a rough circle around him.

'So. We have a proud woman.' Eyes baffled, bored, or attentive settled on him. 'What does *proud* mean?' He hoped a few of them would know—it was a difficult one to explain from scratch. Those who knew would try to explain or quickly translate. He heard the rustle of the words he knew pass around the class: *fier, stolz, orgoglioso*, then something in Arabic and Turkish, words he did not know but would trust. He did the gesture, head high, chin up, looking haughty. Some of the others copied. 'Good. So if *proud* is an adjective, what's the noun?'

'Proudness.' It was always good when a class came up with *proudness*, the pattern-forming a sign that something was sinking in, and then he could shake his head apologetically.

'Good guess, Manuela, but not this time, I'm afraid.'

'Pride,' said Angelika, a German too advanced for this class.

'Exactly! Is pride a good thing or a bad thing?'

'Depends,' said Manuela with a shrug of the shoulders, as if that were an answer.

'On what?' They went through their usual explanations and justifications: it's good to be proud of what you've done, too much is a bad thing.

'A *necklace*? We know what a necklace is.' He pointed to the various ones on display, the girls rolling charms or chains between their fingers. 'And what's a *pearl*?' Never been a problem, this. There was always an earring or a necklace worn by someone in the class, and if not there were stories people knew already, about oysters, divers, or riches.

'And *twenty years* are twenty years.' A general nod. 'Now,' he went on, 'these are three important things from a *story*.' He laid the emphasis on that last word to let them know what they were in for. 'I know what happens in this story, but I think you don't. Is that right?'

Here was the tricky moment. If anyone knew, the activity would be ruined, but today he was lucky: they all shook their heads.

'Good. Now, what you have to do is ask me questions to find out what happens in this story. You can ask me any question at all, anything you like, but I can only answer yes or no.' They groaned, but began.

'Is the woman twenty years old?' Always the first question, this one. He noted Angelika's downward intonation, good pronunciation; she thought this was a cert.

'No,' he replied. A slight bafflement, but no matter, the questions continued.

'Why is the woman proud?' Ayman hadn't been listening.

'Yes or no.' Ayman looked around for help, then went back to flicking through his phone.

'Is the woman married?'

'Yes, she is.'

'Is her husband rich?' asked Venelin, a permanently angry Bulgarian obsessed with money and its lack. Venelin would enjoy this story, he thought.

'No, teacher . . . *was*!' Nour, the Saudi woman, looked at him with dubious eyes.

'Good point, Nour—but when we tell a story we can use the past simple or the present tense.' And he wondered, what *was* the right tense to tell a story in?

'*Allora* . . . is her husband rich?'

'No, he isn't.'

'Does anybody died in this history?'

'Get the question right, Javi.'

'Eh? Oh. Does anybody *die* in this history?'

'Better . . . but . . .?' He looked around the class for help, but none was forthcoming. 'Okay, what's the difference between *history* and *story*?' One was real, the other invented. He wasn't sure if that was true or not, but Venelin's definition would do for now. 'So, Javi?'

'Does anybody die in this story?'

'No.' Disappointment. They always liked death in a story.

'Does the woman have a lover?'

'That'd be an interesting story, wouldn't it, Manuela? But I'm afraid it's not this story.'

'Where does this story happen?'

'Yes or no, Ayman.'

'Is there a murder?' The others joined in, told Brazilian Alex they'd already answered that question, more disappointment. If it began to drag he'd give them clues, an extra word or two—'grand ball,' perhaps, or 'rich cousin.'

'Is the necklace magic?' He loved this question, watching the group all forming their own stories, moving the elements around, slotting them in and out of place where they did or didn't fit.

'No, I'm afraid not.'

'Is there any magic in this story?'

'No.' His turn for disappointment this time: magic gave a told tale a lift you had to work harder to achieve with only solid realist blocks. There'd be mileage in a magic necklace.

'Is—no, *does* the proud woman . . .'

Everyone paused, waiting for Ayman to finish.

'I can only answer complete questions!' Ayman gave up, went back to his phone.

'Is the pearl necklace of the woman?'

'How do you mean, Manuela?

'Does the woman *own* the pearl necklace?'

'Good question!' He had to fudge a bit. 'Yes . . . *and* no.' They laughed, he was bending the rules, but they were intrigued.

'Did she *steal* the pearl necklace?'

'No.' But they were getting closer now.

'Did she borrow the necklace?' Stefan, the quiet Swiss boy with good vocabulary.

'Yes, she did!' They practiced the word *borrow,* and he made sure they also knew *lend.*

'Did she lose the necklace?'

'Yes. She did.'

'Is the necklace real?' They were too warm now: though he had encouraged them, they weren't supposed to get it. There was a delicate art to leaving it just long enough, letting them get close enough, but not quite.

'Yes,' he fudged again, not quite lying. 'It's a real necklace.' He saw a glimmer of something in Stefan's eyes, a memory, perhaps, or the slow logic of possibility sliding into place. 'Do you want to hear the story?' he asked the whole class, trying not to sound too urgent. The timing was important: tell it too soon and you haven't built up enough interest, too late and he risked boring them or running out of time. They assented groggily, apart from Nour: there was always one who'd be dogged enough to go on asking questions, too proud to let the mystery defeat them. 'Do you want to hear the story?' Louder this time, eliciting a louder response, a technique he'd seen a Caribbean storyteller use.

'Yes!' they shouted, Ayman putting his phone under his desk, even Nour shrugging assent, and he started to tell the story.

'This story,' he began, 'takes place one hundred and fifty years ago . . . What year was it a hundred and fifty years ago?' He watched them stumbling with the maths, counting on fingers, amazed how often they got it wrong.

'1963?'

'Really?'

'1863.'

'*1863*, yes. Thank you, Stefan. And it takes place in *Paris*. What was Paris like in 1863?'

'Horses and carriages.'

'Ladies in long dresses.'

'Champs-Élysées.'

'Is it a big city or a small city? A rich city or a poor city?' Depending on the level of the class he could push this further: today's lot were only low intermediate, so he had to keep it essential.

'Big city.'

'Rich and poor.'

'We are in Paris, in 1863, a big city where there are many rich people and many poor people.' He hadn't read the story for years, could hardly remember it, and had told it so often now he'd embellished and changed it and, if there was someone who knew the story, often had to apologise for his liberal retelling. 'Our story starts with a man who is neither very rich nor very poor, but just in the middle, a man who is thankful because he has a job, but it is not an interesting job. He sits in an office, every day, copying piles of documents.' For example, he'd added bits of Gogol's 'Overcoat,' just for flavour.

The story went on almost mechanically, the sequence and details in a memory. By chance the man gets an invitation, a *grand ball*, he's very happy—why? The group came up with their suggestions, he'd get a chance to meet somebody, of course, and then the reveal that he's married, and who's he married to?

'A woman who is very, very *proud*,' and now they all know the word, and the main character is ready. Other tales he'd sometimes forgotten or fluffed, left out important details and seen students walking out looking baffled, but he was on solid ground here. 'But of course she says she can't go—why not?' And again he was always amazed at how they got there, straight away, in every country, in every different culture he'd worked in over his own *twenty years* of teaching, the women above all.

'She has nothing to wear!' They all laughed, and so he went on—the husband gets all the money they have and hands it over to her and she goes out and buys herself the most incredible dress she can find.

'What's it like?' he asked, and works their replies into his telling. 'A long dress. What's it made of?' A good chance to introduce the word *silk* or *satin*. He would leave space for them to improvise, the colour, the style, the accessories. Let them own the story too.

The story went on: She still can't go, because now she has no *jewellery* and no money to buy anything. He'd tell of the rich cousin, then the lend, the eventual grand ball, how the woman turned heads on her entry and danced with everyone she could. He'd had to be careful sometimes: though a group of Palestinian women in Lebanon had loved the story (one of his own proud moments, when he'd received a note from one of them at the end of the course: *The story of the braud woman very beautiful*), a group of Turkish secondary schoolteachers had been shocked at the mention of a woman dancing with other men and drinking champagne.

'And then, at the end of the night when the candles are starting to go out and the carriages are arriving to take people home, only then does she notice . . . she's lost it!'

Every time he told the story, it was always different and always the same. Sometimes people wanted to record his stories, but he wouldn't let them. Each telling was unique, a bond between himself and the listeners, the story not his own, or theirs, or even Maupassant's anymore.

'What does she do?'

She could confess to her cousin and it'd all be over, but she won't, of course, because then there'd be no story: they knew this, and came up with their suggestions.

He loved listening to them, though, and loved telling this story. Not a hack, then, but an entertainer. And there was nothing wrong with this: he liked the idea of writers peddling stories, the lineage of O. Henry and Ring Lardner, men with battered hats and tobacco-stained fingers, hangovers and deadlines.

'She buys a fake!' said Manuela, too close again.

'No. She doesn't do that.'

'She kills herself!'

'No death in this story, Stefan.' He went on, telling of how she goes out again into Paris, but this time not in search of a dress but of a jeweller's where she finds another necklace, exactly the same as the one she had lost, his voice slowly pattering out the lulling rhythm of the sentence. Venelin's eyelids were hanging heavy, he needed to speed up. A ringtone woke the semi-sleeping boy, everyone checked their pockets, bags.

'Ayman!'

'Sorry, teacher!' It was a hazard of everyday life, it didn't bother him anymore. Perhaps other voices from afar should take part in the story too, even if it was only Ayman's boss telling him he had to work an extra shift in the kebab shop this weekend.

'But what's the problem with this necklace?'

'It's false!' Angelika had picked up the idea from Manuela, risky at this point. He shook his head quickly and rubbed his thumb and forefingers together, an international gesture.

'That's right. It is very, very expensive—and she has no money . . . so what does she do?' He could see Angelika and Stefan working now: those who half remembered the story were the worst, risking dropping the bomb of the ending before the target had been reached, so he hurried on to the moneylenders, the debts, the *twenty years* of grinding poverty and hard work to pay them off, going through the words automatically, this part of the story well-rehearsed, mechanical, even risking boring them, they had to get the idea of the sheer length of the woman's misery, the continually turning screw of fate, the terrible result of her own choices bearing down on her.

'And then, twenty years later, she's walking along a street in Paris, no longer proud but old and worn-out and broken, and who does she see coming the other way?' And again, they always knew who it would be. 'That's it! Her rich cousin . . . and she thinks to herself, "I'm not proud anymore, I'm going to tell my cousin what really happened all those years ago."' And the story winds on, inexorable, she retells her tale, and the cousin's face falls as she too tells her terrible truth.

There was always a small silence, just one beat, he left it there, then drew an imaginary line.

'And that's the end of the story.'

There were the usual reactions, wide eyes, horrified laughter. The one person—Ayman, this time—who didn't quite get it or was distracted or whose English wasn't quite as good desperately trying to find out why the others were so startled. Manuela looked delighted, Angelika justified, Nour angry, cheated somehow. A fair response, he thought.

He looked at the clock and realised there were still nearly ten minutes before the end of class. He'd gone too quickly: the perfect timing was when he could leave them with that last line, then get up and leave. Today there'd have to be the discussion. Sometimes he'd ask if they'd ever borrowed anything and lost or broken it; what had they done? He'd borrowed this story, he thought, hoped he hadn't broken it. And sometimes there'd be the question he hated: today, Nour asked it.

'What is the moral of the story?'

'Does a story have to have a moral, Nour?' She didn't reply, but he could tell she didn't like what he was thinking. He wanted to say he thought a story should have an *immoral*, that the best stories upset us and disturbed the world around us, but it wasn't the place, and there wasn't the time.

'Teacher, Sir—need to go!' Ayman didn't wait for permission but got up and ran from the class, ever-present phone in hand. Early start on the doners, he surmised.

He could swerve the discussion, ask them what happened next, though he disliked this too, knowing the perfection of the story lay in its decision to finish just there. He didn't want the argument with Nour so he stood up, checked the clock, and let them go. It was Friday afternoon, no one would worry about a stolen five minutes.

He went straight to the poky staff room, chucked his register on the shelf, grabbed his coat, and made to leave, hoping for an early exit and to avoid seeing the Director on the way out. He wouldn't bother with that story again, would try something more challenging next time, though he realised he might not be able to make that gesture of the invisible line with his hands and say the words *That's the end of the story*, because it wouldn't be: the best stories don't end.

He gathered up his mood with his bag and coat and sped off, down the stairs, across the hall, out of the door, and into the clear, cold air. Friday, weekend. He dug in his pocket for his own phone, wanted to text some friends, hit a bar tonight. He saw Ayman standing on the corner, his phone stuck to his ear, looking anxious, and thought about shooting past with a nod but Ayman waved to stop him. *Damn*, he thought, he didn't want a question about grammar or even the story right now.

'Teacher,' said Ayman, 'Sorry, but my father, seriously ill.'

'I'm sorry to hear that,' he replied. 'Don't worry if you can't make it on Monday,' he went on blithely, knowing well the Border Agency would be on Ayman like a ton of bricks if he missed any more classes.

'Sorry to miss class, but my father, very bad, very bad.' Pity held him, he couldn't run off now.

'Can you go back and visit him?' Ayman screwed up his face and shook his head.

'No, is very difficult. Very difficult.'

'Too expensive?' Ayman shook his head again.

'Not that.' There was something else Ayman wanted to say, but there were no words, only an awkward shuffle. 'My father,' he went on, shifting from foot to foot, 'In jail.'

'I see,' he said, feeling how futile his words were. Ayman held
up his hand in protest, phone still clinging to it.

'But not a bad man, no. Not a bad man.' He stopped moving,
hung his head, then looked up again with an unexpected smile. 'My
father—*proud* man! Very proud!' They both laughed. 'In Turkey,'
continued Ayman, then stopped and winced again. '*Politics*. In Turkey, very...' He sucked in the air between his teeth, searching for an
English word he didn't know.

'Will your father...?' This time he found himself unable to
finish the question. Ayman shook his head.

'Maybe he will not...' And he thought, perhaps this was the
right tense for a story, not the past or the present, but the future.
Ayman stuck out his hand, palm down, and moved it side to side, a
gesture that showed a story far from finished, and of which no one
knew the outcome.

WHAT REMAINS OF CLAIRE BLANCK

A NEW AND ANNOTATED TRANSLATION
OF GREGOR NILZ'S STORY

1

2

---

1   This opening line is a perfect example of beginning as gently extended
hand, an invitation to follow the teller into the unknown. It is a promise upon which the story then delivers.

2   Despite the expanse of this story, throughout we see incredible attention to detail, an interest in the minutiae, the tiny things, the footnotes.

3

4

---

3   The meeting of the two strangers on the deserted street here is—I feel—where the story really begins. Though we are yet early in the narrative, the tension is palpable. What is unsaid (clearly, a lot!) is as important as what is said.

4   The realisation that the street is actually a bridge is perfect in its oneiric specificity.

5

6

7

8

_____

5   Time, as we shall see, is as important as space in this story. Despite its brevity, this story encompasses centuries.

6   Bold technique is the key to this achievement: in this sentence, for example, it is not clear how much time has passed.

7   Though this is a story of loss, it is also one about connections. (The bridge, of course, is the ultimate symbol of both division and connection.)

8   The whiteness here captures the idea that despite the vagueness of a nonspecific geographical location, we are clearly in Arkhangelsk, Murmansk, or Svalbard.

9

10

There again, the quality of the prose here makes me think of nothing more than a foggy day in London, Brussels, or Milan.

10 While this passage is stubbornly opaque, we must remember that the short form, inevitably, means a writer has to edit, omit, delete.

11

12

13

---

11 Such editing, omitting, and deleting means that form and content become indivisible. All short stories are about loss.

12 Here, for example, form becomes content: the account of the loss of the
key may be the story's vital turn.

13 While everything may seem to be vanishing, in this section I can almost
hear the footsteps and their deliberate approach.

14   15

16

---

14   The painting mentioned here is crucial to the story; we cannot be sure
     quite what it is, but I feel certain it is Malevich's 'White on White,'
     one of Piero Manzoni's achromes, or even Rauschenberg's 'White
     Paintings.'

15   A rare word that can mean: 1. The sadness of sad things; 2. Their absurd-
     ity; 3. Our indifference to them.

16   I wonder if there is a word missing here (or maybe more than one).

17

18

19

20

·

---

17 In his *Six Memos for the Next Millennium*, Italo Calvino speaks of the qualities of lightness, quickness, exactitude, visibility, and multiplicity. This section displays all of these, as well as a further one I can only define as *evanescence*. I can think of no other story that has quite this quality of disappearing.

18 The movement here, from thick fog into snow then a raging blizzard, is breathtaking. There is no finer example in all meteorological literature.

19 The dreamlike quality of the piece is here seen again, as the bridge becomes a train carriage.

20 (I must here apologise for the number of footnotes, which, I hope, are not distracting the reader but merely offering a knowing hand to hold as we pass across the apparently simple yet ultimately treacherous surface of icy crystals of this text. A careful exegesis and a trusted guide are nothing but help.)

21

22

23

---

21 Even after reading this story more than a hundred times, I still find this section baffling, and wonder if there is something that I am missing.

22 In German ghost stories, the Weiße Frau is a revenant ancestor, come to warn. We have noted that all stories are about loss, but more, perhaps, about the traces things leave behind. All short stories are ghost stories.

23 A perfect example of this writer's scrupulous meanness, their linguistic economy. Fans of modishly sparse writing should all be made to read this.

24

---

24 In certain Asian cultures, I have been told, white is the colour of mourn-
    ing. In the West, white is often held to symbolise purity, but not here.
    White is nothing more than absence, though it is present throughout.

25

26

27

28

---

25 Other writers give you stories that lengthen or broaden, a few will give
you ones that deepen, but only here do we have an example of a story
that seems to etherealise the moment we read it.

26 I, too, have taken this train. Unlike our narrator, however, I alighted at
a station that was very different.

27 A railway station is, of course, the ultimate point of connections and
losses.

28 Here we are directed back to the story's title, and once again I ask myself
if it should not conclude with a question mark.

29

30

---

29 The sixth of January.

30 Apophenia is the mental condition in which the sufferer sees every-
    thing as being connected. For the apophenic, everything—no matter
    how slight or subtle—is a sign that links to another, and another, and
    another, all leading to a clarity of the whole.

31

32

31 Every great story has one line that is its heart, its vital essence concentrated in but a few words, its lambent core. This is that line. This is the one line that illuminates everything, that lets us feel the story, a story of things that flicker, things that fade.

32 The dazzling bright light here, the transformation or transfiguration, is sublime and terrifying.

33

34

---

33 Knowing what we know now about Gregor Nilz's demise (which is still, alas, all too little), the reader cannot help but wonder if they had foreseen their end, or—indeed—brought it into being.

34 Many stories end with an epiphany, a moment of revelation or understanding, a lifting of the veil. This story offers us no such consolation. Instead, it ends with an apophany.

HENRI BERGSON
WRITES ABOUT TIME

Henri Bergson sits at his desk in a modest house on a quiet street near the Porte d'Auteuil and tries to measure a moment. The clock ticks, the light through the window slats stretches across the floor, barely perceptible. The desk extends to the wall, a flat plane piled with the slow accumulation of his life. He cannot see where the desk ends and the wall begins. A blank sheet of paper lies before him.

He begins to write. The words come without ease, his black, crabbed handwriting crawling slowly across the page. He has not thought clearly enough: he needs to think more carefully, to have his ideas clear, before he can begin to write. He wonders if thought precedes word, or word precedes thought.

Henri Bergson is bored, and wonders if more coffee will redeem his situation. He rings the bell to call the maid and immediately forgets he has done so. The second he tries to measure the instant, the instant is gone. You can measure a line, he realises, because a line is complete and immobile, but time is neither of those. Better try measuring the wind, or using a ruler to measure the sun.

Marie arrives with coffee. She puts a cup on the desk, raises the pot, and begins to pour. Henri Bergson watches carefully: the emptying pot, the filling cup, the spout of coffee in midair. He feels he could be watching for hours, but knows that it is only seconds before the spout twists awkwardly and hits the rim of the cup, upsetting it, sending coffee spilling across the desk, the white sheet of paper, his lap. He jumps up, not yet scalded, Marie drops the pot, which lands on the carpet and does not break, only spills its last few dregs.

'Monsieur!' cries Marie.

'It is nothing, it is nothing,' insists the philosopher, frantically dabbing at himself. 'Go and fetch a cloth or something.' Marie runs from the room in tears.

Henri Bergson sits at his desk and feels time speeding up and slowing down. He looks at the clock on the wall and realises that time is doing neither, but measures out a ponderous steadiness. He knows time is immeasurable, but tries anyway.

Although Henri Bergson does not yet know it, the apex of his career may have passed, even though he is yet to win the Nobel Prize (for literature, not physics). A year ago, Henri Bergson met Albert Einstein at the Société française de philosophie in Paris to discuss the meaning of relativity. The meeting, for Bergson, at least, was not a success.

Henri Bergson hardly hears the knock on the door of his study and the maid entering, noticing only a large cup of strong black coffee appearing on his desk. He wonders why his trousers are damp and cooling.

The memory of the debate still rankles. He had wanted to

talk about science; the scientist, about philosophy. He said Henri Bergson didn't understand physics; Henri Bergson knew he hadn't understood philosophy. Henri Bergson hadn't wanted to offend anyone, respected the German physicist and his work. He had said so, quite clearly. It was that relativity, he thought, wasn't enough. In that story about the twins, the clocks wouldn't slow. He listens to the clock tick-tick-ticking on the wall of his own study and knows that—regularly wound—it would neither slow nor speed wherever it were placed. But what those twins did, what they thought and experienced, that would surely be different, and that would interfere with their sense of time. The physicist hadn't listened.

When Henri Bergson goes to drink the coffee, it has gone cold. The lack of warmth accentuates its bitterness. He screws up his face and spits it back into the cup. How long had it been sitting there, he wonders, for it to go so cold?

But science and philosophy had different jobs to do, though intricately related: two twins, perhaps, one catapulted into space, the other remaining with his feet firmly upon the Earth. He wonders if he may have an other, a strange twin-like creature out there somewhere, a multiple of himself, experiencing time differently.

Henri Bergson looks at the blank sheet of paper in front of him. He has written nothing, it seems, though the paper is now stained with coffee. He rings for Marie again, and when she arrives he has almost forgotten he had called her.

'Ah, yes, Marie,' he says. 'You have been looking very tired recently. I wondered if you had thought perhaps about taking some time off.'

The maid looks at him with a trace of anxiety.

'But Monsieur,' she says, 'I am not Marie. Marie left last month. I am her cousin, Marianne.'

'You look very alike. Almost as if you were twins.'

'They say so, Sir, yes.'

Henri Bergson looks at the typewriter on his desk. An Underwood Standard No. 5, a gift from his publisher no longer able to read the cramped writing of the manuscripts he now produces due to the arthritis in his hands. He has tried to use it but it hurts his fingers even more than gripping a pen. He was advised to have a secretary and dictate but he does not like anyone else between the flow of his thoughts and the paper. The infernal thing makes a terrible noise, disturbing the silence he needs to write with, the silence regularly punctuated by the clock on the wall. This room, on a quiet street in Paris, is so silent he can hear his own heartbeat marking out his own time, which one day will pass, the beat, usually so slow, now momentarily quickened by that small sip of strong black coffee. The clicks and the clacks of the typewriter were too irregular, punctuating nothing other than the slow speed of his writing: a quick burst followed by long gaps.

There is a knock at the door.

'Come in,' says Henri Bergson. It is the maid.

'Excuse me, Monsieur, I came to clear up the mess.' She points to a broken china coffeepot on the floor.

Henri Bergson looks at the spools of ribbon on each side of the typewriter's barrel. One unravels, time moving to its end, the other collects, accumulating continuously. Were he to remove and unspool it, the one on the right would bear the trace of all the words he had written, however few of them. It would remember as surely as the paper feeding under it remembered. The duration would be homogenous, not reflecting the time that had or hadn't passed under the ribbon's experience of his words. One could take the used part of the ribbon and place it over the empty, unexperienced part, and the two moments would become one somehow, yet the two experiences would be different. Henri Bergson thinks no two moments are ever identical, however much this quiet Monday morning slowly moving into afternoon is so similar to the Monday before, and will be like the Tuesday to follow. Only the Tuesday will be different, even though he will be sitting at his desk, not writing, wondering how long it takes his coffee to go cold, because tomorrow's Tuesday will contain this Monday within it, like the imprint of the letters on the spool. Duration conserves the past. Duration is memory, and tomorrow he will remember how the light moves so slightly differently, at a different angle, longer now, the days beginning to stretch into summer. This moment, now, so different to the one only a second ago, because it bears the knowledge of that moment. The past gets bigger, the future, like the dwindling spool, worryingly smaller.

Henri Bergson looks at the notes he has written on the paper before him and has difficulty deciphering his own handwriting. He has to squint as he reads. 'Did I write this?' he asks himself. 'What was I thinking?' He wonders if some other hand might have come and written the words for him, so alien to him do they seem now. Perhaps he should have some coffee; perhaps he is drinking too much coffee. He calls for the maid.

Henri Bergson tries to measure time and realises time can only be measured in decay. That of his own body, its heartbeat slowing again now, the tired ache in his fingers the signs of decrepitude that will one day, he fears, render him totally immobile. Henri Bergson wonders and worries what, where, and how time is. How can that machine know of time? What does the clock know of what it counts out? Time is something humans have invented to put a measure, a fix, a hold on the infinite chaos of the universe and our lives. Time is in our bodies, and in our consciousness.

He hears a slow knock at the door, almost indistinguishable from the tick of the clock, the beat of his heart. The door opens.

'I'm sorry, Monsieur,' the maid says. 'I have been very tired recently. I shall be taking some time off. My cousin Marianne will be coming instead. I have already spoken to Madame.'

Henri Bergson accepts time as he understands it, and places himself firmly in the midst of duration. Everything that has happened is present here, now, though none of it affects what will come. He has freedom, space, mobility.

Henri Bergson watches the black spout of coffee reach from the pot to the rim of his cup.

'Thank you, Marianne,' he says. 'That will be all.'

Henri Bergson looks at what he has written this morning and wonders how long it has taken him to write this, how long it will take to read, and how long it will be remembered. In this second, Henri Bergson feels himself complete and immobile. Would it be possible, he wonders, to measure my life?

Henri Bergson watches coffee slowly pooling across his desk, staining the white paper, turning his words back into ink.

Henri Bergson sits at his desk and writes about time. He hears the sound of his pen scratching against the page, its lonely voice leaving marks that will one day be all that remains of him. He looks at the light on the floor, the motes of dust in the air, hears the silence between the ticks of the clock. There are no moments; there is no now. Only the past, passed, touching the what-will-be.

ST. AUGUSTINE CHECKS
HIS TWITTER FEED

It's a good office, the one he has, not as good as Jerome's, maybe, he knows that, no lion or anything, but pretty good anyhow with its view of the Med and the rolling hills and ships in the harbour, so he briefly entertains a notion of getting his own lion, and maybe a painting too, and posting that, #hardatworkwithfloofyfriend or something, but quickly changes his mind, that's not his brand at all, he's got to stay on brand, and most of all he's got to get some writing done this morning. Maybe just one little picture, though, of that view, which from here on this cool blue morning is so serene, so beautiful. He pauses for a moment of admiration, then checks his Twitter feed again. Someone working on a new translation of *The Odyssey*, the regular pile-on about the Apocrypha, a lame debate about the value of allegories. Nothing interesting, but he keeps on scrolling, thinking about posting a pic of that view with a semi-ironic #writerslife humblebrag or something. But then he knows that hashtags are so passé anyhow, he hates that blocky symbol and the blue text. Avoid the hashtags, he tells himself, it's not his brand: his brand is serious, though also a little bit playful, he wants to push the boundaries a bit, not respect the conventions, it's got him into some trouble in the past but he's through all that now. Now he's more reflective, and that's what this new work will show, just as soon as he gets down to writing it and stops checking his Twitter feed.

So he's got his favourite stylus and some good paper, not cheap, but worth the investment, and he's ready to go, to get down some of those thoughts he's been having about, oh, you know, the nature of suffering, evil, free will, time, the apocalypse, eternity, that kind of thing, but before he does he's just going to make himself a tisane, he could get someone to do it but it's always better if he makes it himself. He'd love a coffee but it hasn't been invented yet. Maybe he should tweet that! Get a few likes, maybe. It's a big project he's setting out on, he knows, and as he waits for the tea to cool he thinks he should perhaps make a detailed plan of what he's going to write, though there again maybe it'd be best to just sit down and get on with it, hit that page, splurge those words. He's going to tell his life story, at length, with lots of examples, personal examples, true ones, no hiding behind allegories or endlessly reinterpreting myths, and some of it will be true, absolutely, but other bits less so, and he'll include all sorts of other things, too, like essays and philosophy and some bits of criticism maybe. Work it all in. Constantly reflecting on the self that he is creating as he writes. A bit like Twitter, only with much more depth. It's a new thing he's doing, he tells himself, there'll be a whole series, maybe twelve, thirteen books. Should he wait and drop them all at once, or put them out, say, once a year? Build up the interest. Maybe he should ask Twitter what it thinks. Maybe he should just go for a walk.

'Confession time! When I was a kid I stole some pears from a neighbour's tree. I didn't even really want them! What did you do just for the hell of it? #FessUp'

He hits the send button, waits a couple of minutes.

No responses. One like. No retweets.

Have I overshared? But isn't that the point? What *is* the point? Should I ask Twitter that: 'What is the point?' Would that seem too nihilistic? Would that be on brand? Why did no one reply to that tweet? Why would someone like it but not bother to respond? Is forty-two too early to write your life story? Should I put that out on Twitter? Do a poll? Would anyone reply? Would I look foolish? Do I care? Why am I doing this? Is the long form really for me? Is doubt good? Why am I writing? Why am I constantly checking my Twitter feed? How long is a moment? When will this end?

St. Augustine often wishes St. Ambrose were on Twitter, or any socials at all, for that matter, but St. Augustine knows that St. Ambrose is far too good for this and wishes he had the patience and fortitude of his mentor. Ambrose wouldn't get worried about being mistaken for a place in Florida or any number of primary schools, or think about changing his handle to @StAugustine_original, or wonder why he hadn't gotten a blue checkmark. Ambrose wouldn't be bothered by the minor irritations, distractions, and disappointments of this world, and Augustine admires this, while also knowing that he can do nothing but embrace them: he wants to translate all his knowledge and experience and wisdom and his doubts and his sorrow and his joy into words, but he cannot stop checking his Twitter feed.

Evening falls, the day has heated then cooled again, and the sky has turned purple, and St. Augustine still hasn't written a word. It doesn't matter, he tells himself, because there will always be tomorrow, and when tomorrow comes, it will no longer be tomorrow, because there is no tomorrow. There is no past, present, or future; only memory, contemplation, and expectation. St. Augustine picks up his phone and checks his Twitter feed.

WALTER BENJAMIN STARES
AT THE SEA

Walter Benjamin sits on a bench scratching his elbow and staring at the sea. He does not stare emptily: images and memories of other seas he has stared at in his fifty-five years on this earth (as a child, the Baltic; as an adult, the Mediterranean) pile on top of each other as he notes how similar and how different they were to the one he now stares at. He is disappointed in himself when after observing qualities of blueness, stillness, and size, he can come up with nothing better than noting that this one is, after all, more *pacific*.

Walter Benjamin stares at the sea and wishes he had something better to do. Sitting still and staring is something he does often, and is good at, a rare moment of time freed from capital, but he cannot deny that it is, quite simply, boring. Time has never been his friend, but never before has it felt quite such an enemy. He is on the edge of comparing the sea to time but blocks the thought before it turns banal. He thinks he should set out on another book, a long one, but even though he stares peacefully at the Pacific Ocean, he cannot settle for the time needed to concentrate on even the idea of a book and thinks he should instead try to finish the many things he has started. The big book about Paris, for one, but Paris is so distant now. A book about Los Angeles, perhaps, where he currently, unexpectedly, finds himself, staring at the sea, fascinated and bored in equal measure.

A large car pulls up alongside the bench next to him. A man get out, takes a small black suitcase from the passenger seat, puts the case on the bench, then sits down next to it. Walter Benjamin likes to observe but does not like to engage so does not attempt to strike up a conversation with the man who, in any case, is, like him, staring out at the sea, though in a noticeably more agitated fashion. After a few minutes the man gets up again, returns to his car and drives off, leaving the suitcase on the bench.

Walter Benjamin briefly considers taking the suitcase, as if to replace the ones he has lost, but swiftly dismisses the idea. He no longer wishes to be involved in other people's lives. He stares at the sea and wonders if anyone thinks of him anymore. If they did, he thinks, they would imagine him exactly as he is: sitting on a bench, unmoving, staring at the sea. He doesn't talk to many of the old lot anymore. Max, Teddy, Bert. He never really had that much time for them, really, nor they for him. They're trying to make a go of it out here, but Walter thinks he has come as far as he can and can go no further. He stares at the sea. Everyone, said someone, has one big idea or lots of small ones. He stares at the sea and thinks that he had lots of big ideas.

Another car pulls up, and a woman gets out and sits on the

bench next to the suitcase. She is wearing sunglasses and has a scarf pulled around her head to protect her hair from the insistent breeze. She looks out at the sea, then looks over to Walter, but Walter does not meet her gaze. She picks up the suitcase, gets back in her car, and drives off. He thinks again about the suitcases he has lost, and who may have claimed them.

He stares at the sea and cannot stop himself from thinking of what brought him here and remembering the journey variously, perilously. After the scramble over the mountains and the switch in the grubby hotel, he could have taken another long walk to Barcelona and from there boarded a ship bound for safety, or he may have taken a train to Madrid and from there one to Lisbon and stood on a hopeful quay, or a train farther south to Algeciras, then a boat to Tangier, from where he would have travelled to Casablanca and waited, or maybe he never took that route at all, and had got out earlier with an exit visa from France and an entry one to the US, but however he did or didn't get here, slipping away into crowds with documents and papers and passports forged or real, he is here now, sitting on a bench, quite alone, staring at the sea.

Walter Benjamin decides to make use of his boredom and go to the cinema. He goes to the cinema often, and alone, and he loves it. The Picfair, the Movie Parade, the Hollywood, the Vista, the Million Dollar, El Capitan, the Egyptian. The cinema is, as Gorky said, *the kingdom of the shadows* and the best place to vanish for a while.

The walk is long, and no one walks in this city but he will not learn how to drive. He has no ability, no interest, and is far too old. There is no bus service he can discern. As he walks, cars occasionally slow and either regard him warily or offer a lift. The latter he waves away. He wants no charity from strangers.

He loves the cinema but often hates the films. The only ones he likes are the crime films, though not the ones with gangsters but the ones about lonely and desperate men or women trying to find a foothold in life, taking risks, disappearing then remaking themselves. He should write something, he tells himself, about these films, though he knows he never will. He walks into the movie theatre even though the show has already begun. He enjoys watching films this way, walking in halfway through and not leaving at the end of the screening but waiting for the programme to begin again. In this kingdom of shadows everything has already passed, and not yet come.

A woman comes in and sits near him. She puts a bag on the seat next to her (a suitcase, notes Walter, thinking about how all suitcases look the same but never are), then fidgets and looks over her shoulder as if waiting for someone to arrive. No one arrives. The woman opens the case, takes some things from it (Walter cannot see what they are), then leaves in the direction of the restroom. A few minutes later she returns, a different woman. This woman is dark-haired, whereas before she was blonde. This woman is heavily made up and wears a scarf around her neck. She waits a few more minutes, then leaves, not taking the suitcase with her.

Walter Benjamin stares at the screen and thinks he should be a detective. Every corner of this city, he thinks, is the scene of a crime.

Walter Benjamin sometimes wonders what he is doing here and other times if he is here at all. As he leaves the movie theatre and begins the long walk back to his bench overlooking the sea he passes the precinct police station and thinks he should go in and report himself missing. I am Walter Benjamin, he will say, and I am a missing person. There will be the usual confusion, and the desk sergeant will register him as Benjamin Walter. He will then leave and remake himself as Ben Walter, a private detective, or a photographer, or a newspaper drudge, a hack writer of pulp novels or screenplays. Ben Walter could smoke lots of grass and listen to jazz. He could wear a hat.

TO ATHENS

I have a friend who is a middle sister. Two years younger than her elder sibling and three years older than the younger one, she is also the black sheep. Her sisters are both wealthy women, involved in finance, or business, or something like that, while she nurtures children and lives in a small house in the English north. Her sisters have not spoken to each other for over ten years. There was a row of some kind, my friend is no longer sure of the details and suspects that the sisters aren't either. But they argued, and have not spoken since. My friend, however, as sister to both, still speaks to each. Neither the younger nor the older has asked if my friend speaks to the other, but she does, and therefore knows what neither of them know: that even though they have not spoken for so long, and know nothing now of each other's lives, they live on opposite sides of the same London park.

if only it could be, as if it could ever be, between them all a thread winding or a river flowing, a

I have a friend who had an affair with an online exorcist. The affair was brief, and made more difficult by the fact that it took place in the middle of lockdown, as though an affair with an online exorcist would not already be complicated enough.

dream sentence, a half-awake sentence, that would do it, that would work, a sentence all rhythm and sound with its sense and its senses confused, gently sweeping or insistently flowing, a

I have a friend whose brother disappeared. He had been troubled, and though previously placid had started obsessively watching mixed martial arts videos and carrying a knife with him everywhere he went. It has been over seven years now, and even though he has been pronounced legally deceased, she says that every time she visits a big city or attends a crowded event she finds herself scanning faces, still looking, always looking.

liquid sentence, a silver thread, a river all thought and all truth, inexorable and mutable as a memory, remembering those no longer here and the ones yet present but unseen for so

I have a friend who is mostly a rational man, but firmly believes in ghosts. He claims they manifest themselves through smells and sounds, and linger in the places they lived when they had bodily form. He recently married and is now rebuilding a house near the coast. I have not seen him for over two years and have not asked him if the place is haunted.

long, it keeps going and going whether you want it to or not, no stop-
ping, water running through these stories, always there never stopping,
as though it could trace a line, find the thread, the link, the

I have a friend who told me he had a twin sister. I asked if they were
identical. 'Well, she's a girl,' he said, 'and besides that, we're completely different, too.' Much later, I briefly met his twin sister. Indeed, she didn't look like him one bit, and was cold and somewhat
standoffish, unlike my kind, generous friend.

connection, the theme, the way through all these stories, find some way
to work out what they mean, if they should mean anything at all more
than what they are, stories only, after all, no more no less than that,
never stopping, there are always more, never stopping, but rivers sepa-
rate, rivers

I have a friend who is one of seven. He rarely sees his eldest two
brothers, and scarcely knows them. They all suspect there are other
siblings out there, too, ones with a different mother, but they do not
know for certain, and now both their mother and their father (a man
who rarely told the truth) are dead and can tell them nothing.

divide hills and part fields, forge valleys, mark boundaries and borders,
so not like a river, no, more like a bridge which joins which links, a
bridge over which people can cross from one side, one bank, one shore to

another but the things rivers divide aren't always solid not always fixed,
the banks shift

I have a friend who is no longer with us, though I still think of him
in the present tense.

reform, reconfigure, like the river itself, which divides people and towns
and lives, which themselves are shifting, mobile, so a river divides and
connects, and as it connects it divides, like one

I have a friend who grew up in Darwin in Northern Australia, which
was hit by a huge tropical storm when she was small. She has few pos-
sessions, moves house often, and always keeps a bag packed. She fears
losing her mind, like her mother did. She is a keen canoeist.

long sentence, like words, like language, which defines and articulates
and categorises despite itself, contradicting itself, trying to fix what can
never be fixed, always missing something, never clear, not even to itself,
like a memory, like a dream true and untrue, never reliable, always

I have a friend whose elderly parents have moved in near her. Only
not together. They separated when she was young, leaving her—an
only child—to spend her time shuttling between them until her
mother immigrated to Canada when she was a teenager. Now, each

parent lives alone in a small house, five minutes in either direction from where she is.

escaping itself, though it can connect join translate articulate, a sentence that goes back on itself goes back into itself a sentence that contradicts and undermines itself even as it ploughs on unstopping, like a river, one thing after another, like a story, like a river but not a

I have a friend who, one drunk night, told me how many men he had slept with.

river at all because rivers, ongoing, may change and swerve and wear away their banks but rivers ongoing only ever flow in one direction and these memories these tales these records go in many directions and have no past or future but spread outward like an endless plain measureless to man that will only be perceived at

I have a friend who lived near the Jialing River in Chongqing during the floods of 2011. Now she lives in Ireland and worries every time it rains but says, 'I love the sound of it, the sound it makes as it comes down.'

the moment memory touches on them never stopping, going on and not, not like a river at all, the wrong metaphor or simile though metaphors

*and similes are all we have, the only way we can translate, the only
way we can think, no not like a river at all because rivers though their
courses may wind and change and shift, only flow in one direction, and
time goes backward forward sideways*

I have a friend whose mother died when she was seventeen. My friend
and her brothers did not visit the hospital before their mother died,
believing her to be ill but recovering, and were not prepared when their
father came home to tell them the news. As soon as he had told them,
he disappeared, leaving my friend to look after her two much younger
brothers and organize her mother's funeral. The father returned two
weeks later, refusing to say where he had been. Many years later, she
found out that her mother had been dead two days before their father
had told them and when she confronted him with this fact, and that of
his absence at the funeral, her father could say nothing but how much
he had loved their mother, and how he could not cope with her loss.

*outward and loops, doubles back on itself like the telling of a tale dif-
ferent every time it is told, every time it is heard too, so yes like a river
flowing, perhaps, always changing depending on who is listening*

I have a friend who, when she was twenty, fell in love with a woman
much older than herself. This woman had two children and when
my friend moved in with them, the children were kind and accept-
ing, though the son asked his mother, 'Are you a lemon now?'

watching, and where they are, and when they are, like friends who may reappear after years and years and years and make you think how long, how

I have a friend who is the only one of us who hasn't quit smoking. He stands outside on his own now, and says he feels lonely, but will not give up.

long has it been since that last time, and when was the last time, and how will we ever know when the last time is because after all it might be this one, this one now, this one now when I'm telling you

I have a friend who knew a couple who smuggled drugs. They went to the country where they got the stuff, wrapped it up tightly, then either ingested it or shoved it up their behinds. My friend tells me that he watched them when they got back, carefully laying newspaper on the floor of their kitchen, squatting, then sifting through their own shit to find the pellets of cling-filmed heroin.

about what happened and about what I remember, not the same thing like friends who are never the same, some of them, though others are always the same and never change though maybe they do but we don't notice because

I have a friend who is a jobbing actor. Some time back he was one of a company who did theatre-in-education work, touring schools in remote areas. One year, finding themselves a member short, my friend enlisted his father as their extra. His father was well into his seventies by then and not a well man. A lifelong alcoholic and heavy smoker, he found the work arduous. Even though he had only a few lines, he struggled to remember them and disliked the early starts, the lugging around of costumes and props, the long trips by uncertain public transport or uncomfortable transit vans. He used his time offstage to smoke cigarettes in corridors or playgrounds and nip at the half bottle of Bells he always kept in his coat pocket. He ended up doing this for five years, at which point he died. Six people attended his funeral.

we've changed though we might not know how we've changed or how much or in what ways because there are no measures for that sort of thing no way of knowing no way of finding out and it's not like

I have a friend who is an avowed atheist while his father is a vicar. They never argue and have the closest father-and-son bond I have ever known.

a river, no, more like a spool of thread a roll of tape or an old typewriter ribbon and it accumulates and grows fatter on one side as it dwindles on the other and everything is stored there and can make a

I have a friend who, when she was twenty-four, found out that her father was not her biological father. When I asked if this had upset her in any way, she said, 'Not really, because I never much liked him anyway.' Several years later the two had a large and very public row, in the check-in queue at an airport, which ended when the father said to her, 'You have always disgusted me.'

comeback at any moment as it warps and weaves and grows, the spool gets misshapen and a tiny speck of dust piece of grit in it distorts everything else, throws everything off, like layers, imperfectly visible, like looking

I have a friend who collects different versions of the Daniel Johnston song 'True Love Will Find You in the End.' So far he has eighteen and cannot decide which is his favourite.

into a fast flowing stream and trying to see the surface and the bed, even though it's not like a river, not at all, really, but as if one small branch or pebble far up

I have a friend who suffers from periodic bouts of insomnia, sometimes only managing to sleep for two or three hours a night. He has tried quitting caffeine, quitting alcohol, going to bed at exactly the same time every day, buying expensive Egyptian cotton sheets, bathing in oatmeal, having a lavender oil diffuser in the bedroom, fitting blackout curtains, wearing an eye mask and earplugs, taking melatonin pills, taking magnesium pills, and various other remedies, but nothing works. I asked him what it is that keeps him awake at night. 'Anger, mostly,' he said. 'Sometimes fear.'

shifted the whole flow of the thing, like one long sentence, like this one that is trying to speak of what links what connects what joins what holds, of what it is that can be broken and fixed and broken again and fixed again

I have a friend who once took his now ex-wife on holiday to Albania. They had a miserable time there, but my friend still likes to tell the story of how they stayed in a place called the Hotel Friendship. The massive, crumbling hotel was entirely empty apart from themselves and a number of cockroaches. On the fourth morning my friend woke up to find his wife had already left, having surreptitiously booked a rare taxi to take her to the airport, and from there, to Athens.

THINGS THAT FLICKER,
THINGS THAT FADE

This city falls down a hill and halts only once it hits the river, leaving it suspended, mid-collapse, its own internal contradictions arresting it before a further slide should send it splashily into the water. Bricks, glass, plaster, paint, slates, and tiles sparkle and crash, spill and cluster into logic-defying blocks: modest houses, grand hotels, granite statues, chintzy cafés, botanical gardens, monumental clocks, train stations, tram stops, gilded spires, and marble domes come to their rest, balanced by a mad architect's invisible hand, stacked up the slope, stopped by a moment in time. This is a city that, surely, has its sweeping boulevards, its many-fountained main square, and its vivid squalling marketplace, but its soul lies in its alleys, its ginnels and nooks, its tunnels, basements, and back rooms, which will open to those who know, or want to know. This city has its fleapit cinemas and dusty arcades, its darkrooms and artists' lofts, its neglected bookshops, subscription libraries, drinking dens, and backstreet bars, where conspiracies have been hatched and genius forged, where fights, flights, and love affairs have been soundtracked by the rattle of coins, the crackle of fire, the soft flow of tears. The river washes this city's lower border, the sky its upper one. Not far from here, around that bend, perhaps, lies the sea. On certain days, when the weather's right, the smell of salt and rust and diesel and fish will fill these streets. This city is a place that should be arrived in and departed from by steamboat or sailing ship.

'How do you know all this?'

'I don't. I'm making it up.'

Across the river, just visible, a strand of hillside or parkland, scrubby bushes and small knots of thorny trees. This city, we realise, lies on one side only of a curving valley, but the view of the open land stretches out of focus, so it's difficult to be certain. Whether the transpontine bank is wild, the wrong side of town, untamed, and untameable, or merely a huge park, the city's lung, is uncertain as the image cuts out just there, framed by a white border. A path winds down the hillside, toward the river, to a bridge that will cross into the city. Look. Two people walk down the path toward the bridge, their backs to us.

'I can see them, yes.'

Look more carefully and we can see that they are holding hands, and it is this tiny detail, one that we have to squint to see, that reaches out and touches us as subtly and as firmly as they touch each other. We see this entire city, with all its dreams and plots, all its wild stories and filigree lies, but it is the image of those two people, so gently entwined, that punctures us.

It's nearly nightfall.

'Not dawn?'

'Dusk, I think. You can tell by the sky.'

They're about to step onto the bridge, heading home, or out for an evening, or setting off somewhere on the night train. Perhaps they're about to say a farewell.

They were alive, once, those people, whoever they were.

'There should be, there must be, another photograph of this couple, with them in the foreground, a proper portrait.'

'There could be.'

'Somewhere.'

But right now we can't know that because the picture is turned over and we see the message written, longhand, on its obverse. There is a stamp in the corner, too, but it has not been franked. Perhaps this postcard was never sent, or was delivered by hand instead. The writing is tiny and in a language that the man holding the card does not speak but knows well enough to read.

So read it he does, then smiles, then puts it back in the box between dozens of others, then walks off, into the crowd of this Sunday morning market, where he soon disappears. The frame pulls out, wide view now, inviting us to enter, to join the crowd, to follow him perhaps and find where he has gone and why he smiled like that and what he knows that we don't, or to marvel at the hundreds of others who will all have their own such tales to tell before they too begin to disperse among those streets that seem so familiar, perhaps because they are the streets of the city shown in the picture on the postcard the man just put back in the box, but we can't do that, not right now, because right now the music swells—

'Are we thinking gentle strings, or a massive banger?'

'I don't know. Which would you prefer?'

'Can't we have both?'

'Sure. I'll leave it up to you.'

—and the closing titles start to roll, the screen slowly darkens as the lights come up and the audience file out, leaving us alone, just me and you.

'Is it time to go?'

'Not yet. Let's wait a bit. See what happens.' I reach out and touch your hand.

ACKNOWLEDGMENTS

Early versions of some of these stories appeared in *Gorse, Lighthouse, The Lonely Crowd, Short Fiction in Theory and Practice* and *3AM* magazines, while others were published by Comma Press, Galley Beggar, and Daunt Books.

'Everything is Subject to Motion' takes its title from a poem by Simon Perril; 'One Art' from another by Elizabeth Bishop. 'Ognosia' is a term coined by Olga Tokarczuk, rendered in English by Jennifer Croft.

Ailsa Cox and Rodge Glass provided invaluable support, encouragement, and suggestions.

To all of them, many thanks.

And, mostly, to Dr. Michelle Devereaux for illuminating so much more.

ABOUT THE AUTHOR

C. D. Rose is an award-winning short-story writer and the author of *The Blind Accordionist*, *The Biographical Dictionary of Literary Failure*, and *Who's Who When Everyone Is Someone Else*. He lives in Hebden Bridge, England.